UNLOCK THE SECRETS OF THE SHARE MARKET

A STRATEGIC GUIDE TO TRADING SUCCESS

PANDIAN P

Table of Content

Preface

Dear Reader,

Welcome to *"Unlock the Secrets of the Share Market: A Strategic Guide to Trading Success,"* an exhaustive resource designed for both novice and experienced traders. The book blends technical analysis, strategic planning, and psychological insights to offer a holistic approach to day trading. Each chapter delves deep into critical aspects of trading, providing readers with practical knowledge and actionable strategies to succeed in the fast-paced world of day trading.

Comprehensive Coverage: The book covers every aspect of day trading, from basic concepts to advanced strategies, making it a valuable resource for traders at all levels.

Risk Management Focus: Emphasizes the importance of risk management and provides detailed guidance on protecting trading capital.

Psychological Aspects: Addresses the psychological challenges of day trading and offers techniques for maintaining emotional control and discipline.

Actionable Strategies: Each chapter includes actionable strategies and tips that readers can immediately implement in their trading routines.

Beginners: Those new to day trading who need a thorough introduction to the basics.

Intermediate Traders: Traders with some experience looking to make consistent profit from the stock market.

Advanced Traders: Experienced traders seeking advanced techniques and a deeper understanding of market mechanics.

Students and Educators: Those studying finance, economics, or related fields who want practical insights into day trading.

Unlock the Secrets of the Share Market: A Strategic Guide to Trading Success is a must-read for anyone serious about succeeding in the competitive world of day trading. By offering a blend of technical knowledge, practical strategies, and psychological insights, this book provides a comprehensive roadmap to achieving trading mastery and long-term success. Whether you're just starting or looking to elevate your trading skills, this book is an invaluable resource on your journey to becoming a successful day trader.

Sincerely,

PANDIAN P

Chapter 1

Understanding Day Trading Fundamental

INTRODUCTION

What is Day Trading?

Day Trading involves buy and sell stocks and financial instrument within the same trading day. Day traders aim to capture on small price movements in higher liquid markets stocks, future, and options. Day trading requires some important skills like Technical Analysis, Money Management and Trading psychology. Many new traders don't bother about these skills they directly jump into the day trading.

Because of that careless reason, 90 percent of day traders lose money in the day trading activity in the stock market, a recent survey noticed. If anyone wants to become an engineer, it will take 4 to 5 years of studies before he masters the relevant field. Unfortunately, in day trading, without any learning, they start their trading, which is a big concern. In my opinion, a minimum of 6 months to 1 year is needed to understand the price movements and market behaviours. In the first year, you have to use minimum capital like 5k or 10k only for learning purposes. Once you learn and gain confidence, you can bring more money into the market.

Strategies, Money Management, Trading Psychology and Trading Journal these 4 skills are like 4 pillars of day trading. These are very essential in day trading. If anyone can followed these 4 skills in their trading system they can surely make consistent return from stock market. In upcoming chapters we can see these 4 important skills and a trader facing difficulties and solutions elaborately.

Key Characteristics of Day Trading

1. **Short Holding Period**:   Day traders open and close positions within the same trading day, ensuring that no positions are held overnight. This helps to avoid the risks associated with overnight price gaps.

2. **High Frequency of Trades**:   Day traders typically execute multiple trades in a single day to exploit small price movements. This can involve dozens or even hundreds of trades daily.

3. **Technical Analysis**:   Day traders rely heavily on technical analysis, using charts, patterns, and indicators to make trading decisions. They often use intraday charts (e.g., 1-minute, 5-minute, 15-minute) to identify trading opportunities.

4. **Leverage**:   Many day traders use leverage to amplify their potential returns. This involves borrowing capital to increase the size of their trades. However, leverage also increases the risk of significant losses.

5. **Liquidity**:   Day traders focus on highly liquid markets and securities to ensure they can enter and exit positions quickly without affecting the market price.

6. **Market Hours**:   Day traders operate during regular market hours from morning 9 am to evening 3.30 pm.

COMMON DAY TRADING STRATEGIES

1. Scalping

This strategy involves making numerous small trades to profit from tiny price changes. Scalpers aim to 'scalp' small profits repeatedly throughout the day.

2. Momentum Trading

Day traders using this strategy look for stocks or other instruments that are moving significantly in one direction on high volume. They aim to ride the momentum for as long as it lasts.

3. Range Trading

This strategy involves identifying key support and resistance levels and buying at the support level while selling at the resistance level. Range traders expect the price to stay within a defined range.

4. Breakout Trading

Day traders look for assets that are breaking out of a defined range or pattern. They enter a trade when the price breaks through a significant level of support or resistance.

5. Reversal Trading

This strategy involves identifying potential reversal points where an asset is expected to change direction. Reversal traders often look for overbought or oversold conditions.

TOOLS AND RESOURCES FOR DAY TRADING

1. Trading Platforms

Advanced trading platforms with real-time data, charting tools, and fast order execution capabilities are essential for day traders.

2. News Services

Access to timely news and information can provide an edge in anticipating market moves.

3. Indicators

Common technical indicators used in day trading include moving averages, pivot levels, Bollinger Bands, RSI (Relative Strength Index), and MACD (Moving Average Convergence Divergence).

4. Risk Management

Effective risk management techniques, such as setting stop-loss orders and position sizing, are crucial to limit potential losses.

RISKS AND CHALLENGES

1. High-Risk

The high frequency of trades and use of leverage can lead to significant losses, especially for inexperienced traders.

2. Emotional Stress

Day trading requires quick decision-making and can be emotionally taxing due to the fast-paced nature of the market.

3. Costs

Frequent trading incurs higher transaction costs, including commissions and fees, which can eat into profits.

Summary

Day trading is a demanding and high-risk strategy that requires significant skill, discipline, and resources. While it offers the potential for quick profits, it also comes with substantial risks. Successful day traders typically have a deep understanding of the markets, a well-defined trading plan, and effective risk management strategies.

MESSAGE OF A CANDLESTICK

What is a candle?

In trading, a candle refers to a graphical representation of price movement over a specific time period like 5 min, 10 min, 15 min, etc. Each candle typically displays 4 crucial pieces of information: the opening price, the closing price, the highest price reached during the time period (the high), and the lowest price reached during the time period (the low). The body of the candle represents the price range between the opening and closing prices, while the wicks (or shadows) extend from the body and indicate the high and low prices. Candlestick charts are widely used by traders to analyze price action and make a trading day.

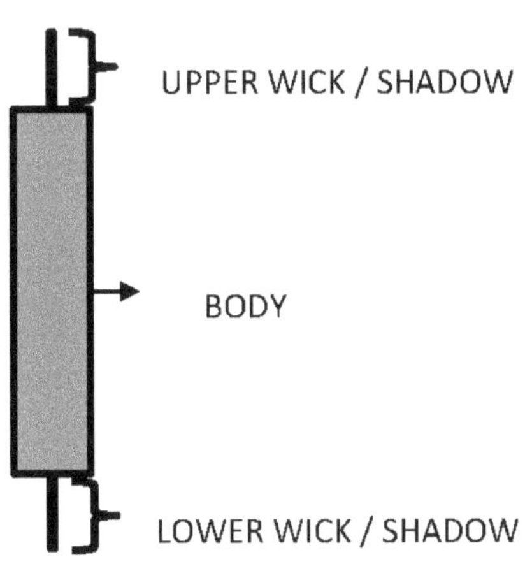

Example of a candlestick

Bullish Candle: When the closing price is higher than the opening price, the body is usually filled with a colour like green or white.

Bearish Candle: When the closing price is lower than the opening price, the body is usually filled with a colour like red or black.

Wicks (or Shadows):   The thin lines extending from the body. They represent the highest and lowest prices during the time period.

Upper Wick: The line above the body indicates the highest price.

Lower Wick: The line below the body indicates the lowest price.

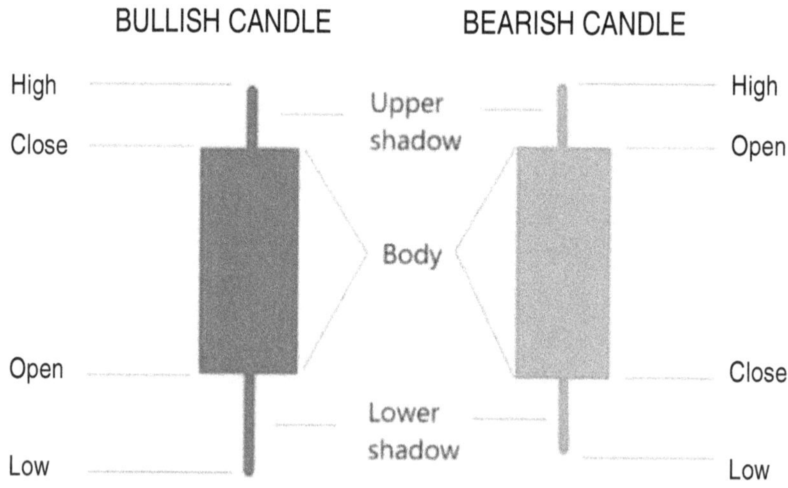

Key Components

Open: The price at which the asset starts trading at the beginning of the time period.

Close: The price at which the asset finishes trading at the end of the time period.

High: The highest price reached during the time period.

Low: The lowest price reached during the time period.

Reversal Candles

A reversal candle pattern signals a potential change of direction of a trend. We can identify extra-long shadow candles called reversal candles or rejection candles. The colour of the candle is red or green, big, or small, that doesn't matter.

The candle shows a shift from bearish to bullish. The bigger lower tail tells us the rejection of lower levels, which shows buying pressure in the market.

The candle shows a shift from bullish to bearish. The bigger upper tail tells us a rejection of higher levels. That shows selling pressure in the market.

Doji or Neutral candles

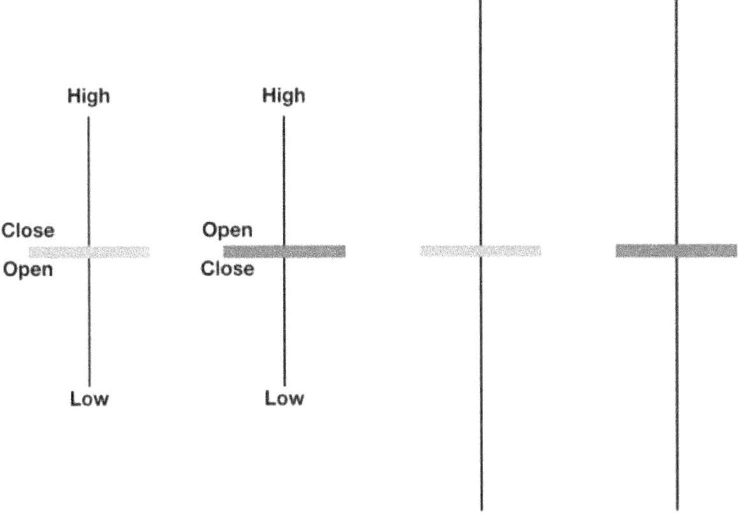

A doji pattern forms the opening price and closing price are nearly equal, in a small body with long upper and lower wick. This shows neutral position in market with neither buyers nor sellers dominating the market. The message is market direction is not yet decided. Always wait for candle let them close than only we can easily identify whether it is a reversal candle or doji candle.

IMPORTANCE OF CANDLESTICK IN TRADING

1. **Trend Identification**:   By observing the patterns formed by multiple candlesticks, traders can identify market trends (uptrend, downtrend, sideways).

2. **Reversal Signals**:   Certain candlestick patterns indicate potential reversals in the market direction.

3. **Support and Resistance**:   Candlestick patterns help in identifying levels of support (price levels where the asset tends to stop falling) and resistance (price levels where the asset tends to stop rising).

4. **Market Sentiment**:   The size and shape of candlesticks can indicate the strength of buying or selling pressure.

THE 2 TYPES OF MARKET DAYS

Everyday market moves are different and unique. We can mostly classify 2 types of market movements.

1. Trending Market
2. Range-bound Market

Trending Market

In trading, a 'trending market' refers to a market that is consistently moving in one direction over a period of time. This can be either an uptrend, where prices are generally rising, or a downtrend, where prices are generally falling. Understanding trending markets is crucial for traders because it helps them align their trading strategies with the prevailing market direction, increasing the likelihood of successful trades. Here are the key concepts related to trending markets:

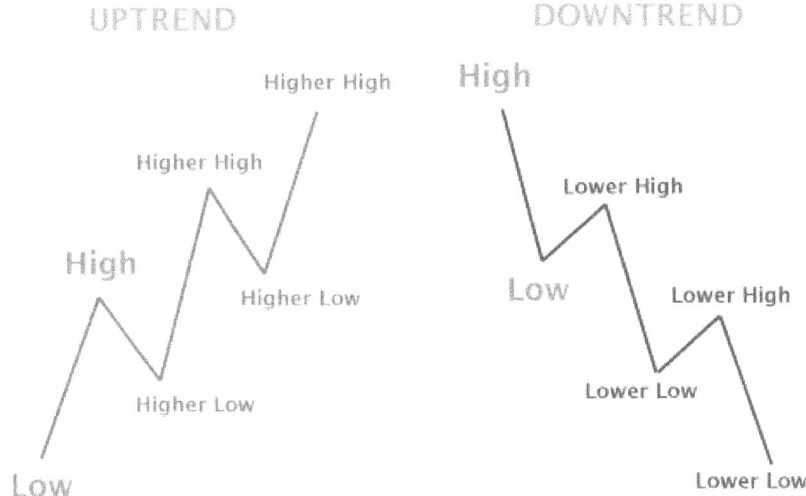

Key Characteristics of a Trending Market

Higher Highs and Higher Lows (Uptrend):

In an uptrend, the market forms higher highs (peaks) and higher lows (troughs).

This pattern indicates a continuous increase in buying pressure.

Lower Highs and Lower Lows (Downtrend):

In a downtrend, the market forms lower highs and lower lows.

This pattern suggests a continuous increase in selling pressure.

Trend Lines:

Trend lines are drawn on charts to visually represent the direction of the trend.

In an uptrend, the trend line is drawn by connecting the higher lows.

In a downtrend, the trend line is drawn by connecting the lower highs.

Trending markets offer clear opportunities for traders to capitalise on the prevailing market direction. By identifying trends through various tools and techniques, traders can align their strategies to buy in uptrends and sell in downtrends, increasing their chances of making profitable trades. However, it's important to combine trend analysis with other technical indicators and sound risk management practices to enhance trading success.

Sideways Market in Trading

A sideways market, also known as a range-bound market, occurs when the price of an asset fluctuates within a horizontal range, showing no significant upward or downward trend. This type of market typically forms when the forces of supply and demand are relatively balanced, preventing the price from breaking out significantly in either direction. Understanding a sideways market is crucial for traders as it requires different strategies compared to trending markets. In 70 percentage of times market sideways range-bound only.

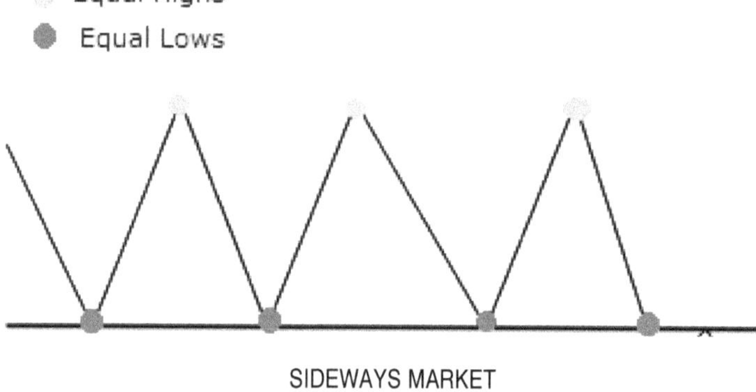

SIDEWAYS MARKET

KEY CHARACTERISTICS OF A SIDEWAYS MARKET

Horizontal Price Movement

Prices oscillate within a defined upper resistance level and a lower support level.

There is no clear long-term trend; the market moves sideways.

Equal Highs and Lows

The price repeatedly touches the resistance level (highs) and support level (lows) but fails to break through either significantly.

Low-Volatility

Compared to trending markets, sideways markets typically exhibit lower volatility.

Price movements are less pronounced and more predictable within the established range.

STRATEGIES FOR TRADING IN A SIDEWAYS MARKET

Range Trading:

Buy near the support level and sell near the resistance level.

Use technical indicators like the Relative Strength Index (RSI) to confirm overbought or oversold conditions.

Breakout Trading:

Prepare for potential breakouts by placing buy orders above resistance and sell orders below support.

Monitor volume closely, as breakouts with high volume are more likely to sustain a new trend.

Options Strategies:

Utilise options strategies such as straddles or strangles, which can profit from a breakout in either direction.

Selling options like covered calls can also be effective in generating income during low-volatility periods.

Summary

Sideways markets present unique challenges and opportunities for traders. By recognizing the characteristics of a range-bound market and employing appropriate strategies, traders can effectively navigate these periods of consolidation. While the potential for significant profits might be lower compared to trending markets, disciplined trading within established ranges can still yield consistent returns. Understanding and adapting to the nature of a sideways market is an essential skill for any trader's toolkit.

Chapter 2

Important Indicators

CPR [CENTRE PIVOT RANGE] IN DAY TRADING

CPR, Centre pivot Range is a well-known technical analysis tool used in day trading. It helps to identify 3 potential supports and 3 potential resistances in your day trading setup. The CPR consists of 3 lines: the top central pivot [TCPR], the Pivot point, and the bottom central pivot [BCPR].

These levels are calculated from the previous day's values. The CPR levels are very useful in day trading. We can use these CPR levels for all stocks as well as all indices like Nifty and Bank nifty also. The 'Central Pivot Range' act as a Magnet. Because most of the time the values reach the CPR or crossover up and down during the market hours.

PIVOT LEVELS

R3

R2

R1

TCPR

CPP

BCPR

S1

S2

S3

CALCULATING CPR LEVELS

Calculate the Centre Pivot Range [CPR]

The pivot point is calculated by using the Previous Day's High [PDH], the Previous Day's Low [PDL] and the Previous Day's Close [PDC].

Centre Pivot Point = {High + Low+ Close}/3

Bottom CPR = {High + Low} / 2

Top CPR = {Pivot point – BCPR} + Pivot point

Sometimes, the Bottom CPR value is above the pivot point. It acts as a Top CPR [TCPR] and vice versa.

Example Calculation

We have taken Bank nifty spot price on 16, May 2024

Day's High = 48052 Day's Low = 47340 Day's Close =47977

Pivot Point Formula = High + Low + Close / 3

$$= 48052 + 47340 + 47977/3$$

Pivot Point	= 47787
Bottom CPR	= High + Low / 2
	= 48052 + 47340 / 2
Bottom CPR	= 47696

If the value is above the pivot point, it acts as a TCPR.

Top CPR	= {Pivot point – BCPR} + Pivot point
	= {47787 – 47696} + 47787
	= 91 + 47787
TOP CPR	= 47878

The same calculation, as well as any stocks, also

On 17th May, we apply these levels to our chart

TOP CPR 47878

CPR 47787   Wide CPR

BOTTOM CPR 47696

If the CPR range is wide, most of the time, the next-day, Bank nifty will be sideways [Range-bound] day.

WIDE CPR

NARROW CPR

If the CPR range is narrow, the next-day market will be trending day most of the time, not all times

Example CPR calculation for stocks

I have taken SBIN stock on 15 May 2024

High = 825 Low = 818 Close = 820

CPP   = High + Low +Close / 3

                             = 825 + 818 + 820 / 3

CPR   = 821

Bottom CPR/Top CPR   = High + Low / 2

                             = 825 + 818 / 2

TOP CPR = 821.50. See, the price is above the pivot point, so we consider it as Top CPR.

Bottom CPR   = [Pivot point – TCPR] + Pivot point

                              = [821 – 821.50] +821

Bottom CPR   = 820.50

On 16 May, apply these levels on our chart.

TCPR 821.50

CPP 821

BCPR 820.50

Calculation of Other Pivots [Supports and Resistance]

R3 = R1 + [High – Low]

R2 =Pivot + [High – Low]

R1 = 2* Pivot – Low

TC = [Pivot – BC] + Pivot

Pivot = [High + Low +Close] / 3

BC = [High + Low] /2

S1 =2 *Pivot – High

S2 = Pivot – [High – Low]

S3 = S1 – [High – Low]

[SOURCE: Secrets of a Pivot Boss by Franklin O. Ochoa]

All the calculations are in your trading terminal. These levels are very important for price action traders in the stock market. The above same calculation is for daily pivots for Day trading, Weekly pivots for swing trading, Monthly pivots for Position trading and Yearly pivots for investors.

There are many strategies available for using CPR. If the price trades above the CPR, it's a bullish sign, and CPR acts as a support. Conversely, if the price trades below the CPR It's Bearish sign, CPR acts as a resistance. CPR is one of the powerful indicators in day trading. It gives more ideas about the price action according to the pivot levels, and we can take entry-exit ideas in day trading. Most of the time, CPR is an exit place for professional traders. Because it's a turning point, it takes time to decide the direction.

Pivot points offer several benefits for traders, enhancing their ability to make informed trading decisions. Here are some of the key advantages of using pivot points in trading:

BENEFITS OF USING PIVOT POINTS

Identifying Key Levels

Support and Resistance: Pivot points help identify key support and resistance levels where price movements are likely to occur. These levels can act as entry and exit points for trades.

Simplicity

Ease of Calculation: Pivot points are straightforward to calculate using high, low, and close prices from the previous trading period. This simplicity makes them accessible to both novice and experienced traders.

Market Sentiment

Bullish/Bearish Indicators: The position of the current price relative to the pivot point helps gauge market sentiment. If the price is above the pivot point, it suggests a bullish sentiment; if it is below, a bearish sentiment.

Trade Planning

Entry and Exit Points: Pivot points provide clear levels for planning trades, setting stop-loss orders, and determining profit targets. This helps traders create well-defined trading strategies.

Versatility

Applicable Across Markets: Pivot points can be used in various markets, including stocks, commodities, and forex. They are versatile and effective across different asset classes.

Time Frames

Multiple Time Frames: Pivot points can be calculated for different time frames (daily, weekly, monthly), making them useful for both short-term and long-term trading strategies.

Support for Other Indicators

Complementary Tool: Pivot points can be used in conjunction with other technical indicators such as moving averages, RSI (Relative Strength Index), MACD (Moving Average Convergence Divergence), and more. They provide additional confirmation for trade decisions.

Risk Management

Setting Stop-Loss Levels: Pivot points assist in setting stop-loss levels to manage risk effectively. Traders can place stop-loss orders below support levels or above resistance levels identified by pivot points.

Trend Confirmation

Identifying Trends: By comparing current price action with pivot point levels, traders can confirm the strength and direction of a trend. This helps in making more informed trading decisions.

Summary

Pivot points are a valuable tool for traders, providing clear and actionable information about potential price levels where significant market reactions might occur. Their simplicity, versatility, and ability to complement other technical analysis methods make them an essential part of many traders toolkits. By using pivot points, traders can enhance their market analysis, improve trade planning, and better manage risk.

MOVING AVERAGES IN DAY TRADING

Introduction to Moving Averages in Trading

In the dynamic world of trading, moving averages are one of the most widely used tools by traders and investors alike. These averages are foundational elements of technical analysis, helping to smooth out price data and create a clearer picture of the underlying trend. By eliminating the noise caused by random price fluctuations, moving averages provide a more consistent and reliable indicator of market direction.

What is a Moving Average?

A moving average (MA) is a statistical calculation that averages a set of data points over a specific period of time. In the context of trading, it typically involves averaging the closing prices of a security. This average is then plotted on a chart, forming a line that moves as new data points are added and old ones are removed.

There are several types of moving averages, but the most commonly used are the Simple Moving Average (SMA) and the Exponential Moving Average (EMA):

Exponential Moving Average: This moving averages EMA is more preferable for day trading. This type of moving average gives more weight to recent prices, making it more responsive to new information. The EMA is particularly useful for identifying short-term trends.

Calculating EMA

To calculate 5 days EMA taking the last 5 days closing prices of the stock or any index and divided by 5. This process is repeated for each new day. Every day we dropping the old price and adding the new average of closing price. Similarly we calculate 10 period MA, 20 period MA as well. In day trading this 10 EMA/20 EMA sloping line gives proper entry-exit levels for trending days most of the time.

How Moving Averages are Used in Trading

1. Identifying Trends

Moving averages are instrumental in identifying the direction of the market trend. In day trading, recognizing the trend is crucial as it dictates the overall trading strategy.

Uptrend: When the price is consistently above the moving average, it indicates an uptrend. Day traders may look for buying opportunities during pullbacks to the moving average.

Downtrend: When the price is below the moving average, it signals a downtrend. Day traders might look for selling opportunities during rallies to the moving average.

2. Support and Resistance Levels

Moving averages often act as dynamic support and resistance levels, providing potential entry and exit points for day traders.

Support: In an uptrend, the moving average can act as a support level where prices tend to bounce back up.

Resistance: In a downtrend, the moving average can act as a resistance level where prices tend to reverse downwards.

3. Moving Average Crossovers

One of the most popular strategies among day traders is the moving average crossover, which involves the interaction between 2 different moving averages.

Golden Cross: This occurs when a short-term moving average crosses above a long-term moving average, indicating a potential bullish signal. Day traders might use this signal to enter long positions.

Death Cross: This occurs when a short-term moving average crosses below a long-term moving average, indicating a potential bearish signal. Day traders might use this signal to enter short positions.

4. Intraday Trend Reversals

Day traders use moving averages to spot potential trend reversals within the trading day.

Moving Average Bounces: When the price repeatedly bounces off a moving average but then suddenly crosses and stays on the opposite side, it may indicate a trend reversal.

Divergence: Divergence between the price and a moving average can signal a potential reversal. For example, if prices are making higher highs but the moving average is flattening or declining, it may indicate a weakening trend.

Summary

Moving averages are an essential tool in the trader's arsenal, providing critical insights into market trends and helping to make more informed trading decisions. By understanding how to effectively use moving averages, traders can enhance their ability to predict market movements and develop robust trading strategies. Whether you are a novice trader just starting out or an experienced professional, incorporating moving averages into your trading toolkit can provide a significant edge in navigating the complexities of the financial markets. CPR with moving averages giving edge of day trading.

THE IMPORTANCE OF THE PREVIOUS DAY'S HIGH

In day trading, the previous day's high is a significant price level that traders closely monitor. This level represents the highest price at which a security traded during the previous trading session. Understanding and utilising this key level can provide valuable insights and opportunities for making profitable trading decisions. Here are several reasons why the previous day's high is important in day trading:

1. Key Resistance Level

The previous day's high often acts as a key resistance level. When the market opens, traders watch to see how the price behaves around this level.

Resistance: If the price approaches the previous day's high and fails to break through, it can act as a resistance level, indicating a potential selling opportunity.

Breakout: If the price breaks above the previous day's high, it can signal strong bullish momentum and a potential buying opportunity.

2. Indicator of Market Sentiment

The previous day's high reflects the maximum price that buyers were willing to pay during the last trading session. If the current price action approaches or surpasses this level, it can indicate a shift in market sentiment.

Bullish Sentiment: When the price moves above the previous day's high, it often signifies increased buying interest and a positive market sentiment.

Bearish Sentiment: Conversely, if the price struggles to reach the previous day's high, it might suggest weak buying interest and a potential bearish sentiment.

3. Confirmation of Trends

The behaviour of the price around the previous day's high can help confirm the strength and direction of the current trend.

Uptrend Confirmation: In an uptrend, a break above the previous day's high can confirm the continuation of the trend, encouraging traders to hold or add to their long positions.

Reversal Signal: In a downtrend, failure to break the previous day's high might reinforce the downtrend, prompting traders to consider short positions or hold off on new long positions.

4. Intraday Trading Strategies

The previous day's high is a critical component of various intraday trading strategies, including:

Breakout Strategies: Traders look for breakouts above the previous day's high to capture significant upward movements.

Reversal Strategies: Traders watch for price rejections at the previous day's high to enter short positions or anticipate reversals.

Range Trading: In a ranging market, the previous day's high and low define the boundaries within which traders can buy low and sell high.

Summary

The previous day's high is a crucial level in day trading, serving as a key resistance level, an indicator of market sentiment, a basis for entry and exit points, and a confirmation tool for trends. By incorporating the previous day's high into their trading strategies, day traders can better navigate the market, manage risks, and capitalize on potential trading opportunities. Understanding the dynamics around this level is essential for making informed and strategic trading decisions in the fast-paced world of day trading.

THE IMPORTANCE OF THE PREVIOUS DAY'S LOW IN TRADING

In trading, the previous day's low is a critical price level that traders closely monitor. This level represents the lowest price at which a security traded during the previous trading session. Understanding and utilizing this key level can provide valuable insights and opportunities for making profitable trading decisions. Here are several reasons why the previous day's low is important in trading:

1. Key Support Level

The previous day's low often acts as a key support level. When the market opens, traders watch to see how the price behaves around this level.

Support: If the price approaches the previous day's low and holds, it can act as a support level, indicating a potential buying opportunity.

Breakdown: If the price breaks below the previous day's low, it can signal strong bearish momentum and a potential selling opportunity.

2. Indicator of Market Sentiment

The low prices on the previous days reflect the minimum price that sellers were willing to accept during the last trading session. If the current price action approaches or surpasses this level, it can indicate a shift in market sentiment.

Bearish Sentiment: When the price moves below the previous day's low, it often signifies increased selling pressure and a negative market sentiment.

Bullish Sentiment: Conversely, if the price struggles to reach the previous day's low, it might suggest weak selling interest and a potential bullish sentiment.

3. Confirmation of Trends

The behaviour of the price around the previous day's low can help confirm the strength and direction of the current trend.

Downtrend Confirmation: In a downtrend, a break below the previous day's low can confirm the continuation of the trend, encouraging traders to hold or add to their short positions.

Reversal Signal: In an uptrend, failure to break the previous day's low might reinforce the uptrend, prompting traders to consider long positions or hold off on new short positions.

4. Intraday Trading Strategies

The previous day's low is a critical component of various intraday trading strategies, including:

Breakdown Strategies: Traders look for breakdowns below the previous day's low to capture significant downward movements.

Reversal Strategies: Traders watch for price bounces at the previous day's low to enter long positions or anticipate reversals.

Range Trading: In a ranging market, the previous day's high and low define the boundaries within which traders can sell high and buy low.

Summary

The previous day's low is a crucial level in trading, serving as a key support level, an indicator of market sentiment, a basis for entry and exit points, and a confirmation tool for trends. By incorporating the previous day's low into their trading strategies, traders can better navigate the market, manage risks, and capitalize on potential trading opportunities. Understanding the dynamics around this level is essential for making informed and strategic intraday trading decisions.

Chapter 3

Money Management Techniques

---

1. POSITION SIZING

1. Introduction to Position Sizing

Position sizing refers to determining the amount of capital allocated to a single trade. It's a crucial component of risk management in day trading, influencing potential returns and mitigating losses. Proper position sizing helps maintain a balanced portfolio, prevents significant losses, and ensures sustainable trading.

2. Importance of Position Sizing

Risk Management: Protects capital by limiting exposure to any single trade. Because protect capital is very important in day trading.

Consistency: Promotes disciplined trading and reduces emotional decision-making.

Survival: Ensures traders can withstand losing streaks without devastating their accounts.

3. Basic Position Sizing Strategies

Fixed Amount: Allocating a predetermined amount to each trade. Simple but may not account for varying risk levels.

Fixed Percentage: Allocating a fixed percentage of the total trading capital to each trade. This method adjusts the position size as the account value changes.

4. Calculating Position Size

The basic formula for position sizing is:

Position Size = Account Equity × Risk Per Trade / Trade Risk

Account Equity: Total capital in the trading account.

Risk Per Trade: The percentage of the account equity that a trader is willing to risk on a single trade.

Trade Risk: The difference between the entry price and the stop-loss price.

5. Example Calculation

Suppose a trader has an account equity of Rs 1,00,000 and is willing to risk 1% per trade. They identify a trade with a Rs 2 risk per share (entry at Rs 50, stop-loss at Rs 48).

Position Size = 100,000 × 0.01 [1%] / 2

= 1000/2

Position size = 500 shares.

The trader would buy 500 shares of the stock. This varies from stock to stock.

If one trader trades Index buy options risk for 1% per trade, their entry at Rs 100 and SL at Rs 80

Position size = 100,000 × 0.01 [1%] /20 [risk]

= 1000 / 20 = 50

Nifty lot size 25 so, Trader would buy 2 lots of nifty options with Rs 1 00,000 capital risk of 1% per trade.

Bank nifty lot size 15 so, Trader would buy 3 lots of bank nifty option with 1 lakh capital risk of 1% per trade.

Many trading platforms offer built in tools for calculating position size. Which can automate the process and reduce errors.

b. Psychological Aspects of Position Sizing

Position sizing isn't just a mathematical exercise; it also has psychological implications. Traders must be comfortable with their risk levels to maintain discipline and avoid emotional trading decisions.

1. Adapting Position Sizing to Different Strategies

Different trading strategies may require different position sizing methods. For example, scalpers may use smaller position sizes with tighter stops, while swing traders might allow for larger positions with wider stops.

2. Common Mistakes in Position Sizing

Ignoring Risk Levels: Taking on a position that is too large without considering potential losses. Most of the novice traders making these mistakes often.

Inconsistent Sizing: Changing position sizes arbitrarily without a clear strategy. Once your capital doubled than increase the position size is advisable.

Overleveraging: Using too much leverage can amplify losses and lead to significant drawdowns. Nowadays most of the broker houses not giving leverages.

3. Continuous Improvement

Successful traders continuously refine their position sizing strategies based on their performance and market conditions. Keeping a trading journal to track the effectiveness of position sizing decisions is crucial for ongoing improvement.

Summary

Position sizing is a fundamental aspect of day trading that directly impacts a trader's success and longevity in the market. By understanding and applying sound position sizing techniques, traders can enhance their risk management, maintain consistent performance, and achieve long-term profitability.

2. UNDERSTANDING RISK-REWARD RATIO

1. Introduction to Risk-Reward Ratio

Risk-Reward Ratio is a key to success in intraday trading. I strongly recommend to all traders especially beginners in stock market to follow this RRR it is edge to your trading career. The risk-reward ratio (RRR) is a key metric in trading used to compare the potential risk of a trade to its potential reward. It helps traders assess the profitability and feasibility of a trade before entering a position. A good understanding of RRR can enhance a trader's risk management strategy and improve overall trading performance.

2. Calculating Risk-Reward Ratio

The risk-reward ratio is calculated by dividing the potential loss (risk) of a trade by the potential profit (reward).

In stock market there is no strategy to win rate above 90%. If you have a strategy with win rate of 50% with followed the RRR you can earn consistent money in stock market.

Example Calculation

Win rate 50%

30 Trades per Month

Risk-Reward Ratio 1: 2

Loss 1 % Profit 2 %

10 wins = 15x 2 % = 30 %

10 losses = 15 x 1 % = 15 %

Net 15 % return per month

If the win rate is even 40 %

30 Trades per Month

Risk-Reward Ratio = 1 : 2

40 % win 12 wins 12 x 2% = 24 %

18 Losses 18 x 1 % = 18 %

Net = 6% Return per month.

This is the reason I am saying that the risk-reward ratio is the holy grail in day trading.

3. Importance of Risk-Reward Ratio

Informed Decision-Making: Helps traders make informed decisions about whether a trade is worth taking.

Risk Management: Ensures that trades have a favourable balance between risk and reward, which can improve overall profitability.

Consistent Strategy: Encourages consistency and discipline by setting clear criteria for trade entry and exit.

4. Setting Risk-Reward Ratios

Standard Ratios: Commonly used RRRs in trading are 1:2, 1:3. This means for every Rs risked, the trader aims to make Rs 2, Rs 3, or more.

Custom Ratios: Depending on the trading strategy and market conditions, traders may adjust their RRR to suit their specific needs and risk tolerance.

5. Applying Risk-Reward Ratio in Trading

Identify Entry and Exit Points: Determine where to enter the trade and set stop-loss (risk) and take-profit (reward) levels.

Example: If entering a trade at Rs 100, with a stop-loss at Rs 98 and a take-profit at Rs 104, the risk is Rs 2 and the reward is rest, resulting in a 1:2 RRR.

Use of Technical Analysis: Employ technical indicators, chart patterns, and support/resistance levels to define realistic stop-loss and take-profit points.

Summary

The risk-reward ratio is a fundamental concept in trading that helps manage risk and maximise potential profits. By setting and adhering to appropriate RRRs, traders can improve their decision-making process, maintain discipline, and achieve consistent success in the markets. Regular review and adjustment of RRRs ensure that trading strategies remain effective and aligned with market conditions.

3. COMPREHENSIVE TRADING PLAN

Creating a comprehensive trading plan is crucial for achieving consistent success in the markets. A well-defined trading plan includes clear guidelines for entry and exit strategies, risk management, and overall trading goals. Here is a step-by-step guide to creating an effective trading plan:

1. Trading Goals and Objectives

a. Define Your Goals

Short-term Goals: Daily or weekly profit targets.

Long-term Goals: Annual returns, account growth targets, or specific financial milestones.

b. Set Realistic Expectations

Understand the risks involved and set achievable profit targets.

Focus on percentage returns rather than absolute dollar amounts to maintain consistency.

2. Market Analysis

Fundamental Analysis: Evaluate economic indicators, company earnings, and news events that impact the market.

Technical Analysis: Use charts, indicators, and patterns to forecast price movements.

3. Trading Strategy

a. Define Your Trading Style

Day Trading: Short-term trades, often within a single day.

Swing Trading: Holding positions for several days to weeks.

Position Trading: Long-term trades, holding positions for weeks to months.

b. Entry Strategy

Technical Indicators: Use moving averages, RSI, CPR, Bollinger Bands, etc., to identify entry points.

Chart Patterns: Recognise patterns such as head and shoulders, flags, and triangles.

Price Action: Identify key levels of support and resistance, as well as candlestick patterns.

c. Exit Strategy

Take-profit levels: Set predefined profit targets using technical analysis or fixed risk-reward ratios.

Stop-Loss Orders: Define stop-loss levels to limit potential losses based on technical analysis.

Trailing Stops: Implement trailing stops to lock in profits while allowing for potential gains.

4. Risk Management

a. Position Sizing

Determine how much of your capital to risk on each trade (e.g., 1-2% of your trading capital per trade).

b. Leverage and Margin

Use conservative leverage to manage risk effectively.

Understand margin requirements and maintain a cushion to avoid margin calls.

c.   Risk-Reward Ratio

Ensure each trade has a favourable risk-reward ratio (e.g., at least 1:2 or higher).

5. Trade Management

a.   Real-Time Monitoring

Continuously monitor open positions and market conditions.

b   Adjusting Stops and Targets

Modify stop-loss and take-profit levels based on market movements and new information.

c.   Handling News and Events

Be prepared to react to significant news events that can impact your trades.

6. Record Keeping and Review

a. Trading Journal

Maintain a detailed trading journal to record each trade, including entry and exit points, reasons for the trade, and outcomes.

b.   Performance Metrics

Track key metrics such as win rate, average profit/loss, and risk-reward ratios.

c.   Regular Review

Periodically review your trading journal and performance metrics to identify patterns, strengths, and areas for improvement.

7. Psychological Considerations

a. Emotional Discipline

Stick to your trading plan and avoid making impulsive decisions based on emotions.

b. Stress Management

Practice techniques such as mindfulness, exercise, and adequate rest to manage trading-related stress.

c. Confidence and Patience

Build confidence in your trading strategy through back-testing and paper trading.

Be patient and wait for high-probability trading setups.

8. Contingency Planning

a. Risk Mitigation

Have a plan in place for unexpected events, such as market crashes, technical failures, or personal emergencies.

b. Backup Plans

Use features like guaranteed stop-loss orders, maintain backup internet connections, and have alternative trading platforms ready.

Summary

A comprehensive trading plan is essential for successful trading, providing clear guidelines for all aspects of trading. By defining goals, conducting thorough market analysis, developing effective strategies, managing risk, maintaining discipline, and continuously improving, traders can enhance their chances of achieving consistent profitability in the markets. Regular review and adaptation ensure that the trading plan remains relevant and effective in dynamic market conditions.

4. CUT YOUR LOSSES EARLY

1. Introduction

One of the most critical principles in trading is to cut your losses early. This approach minimises potential losses, preserves capital, and helps maintain emotional and financial stability. Implementing effective strategies for cutting losses can significantly enhance long-term trading success.

2. Why Cutting Losses Early is Important

a. Capital Preservation

Protects trading capital, allowing you to stay in the game and seize future opportunities.

b. Emotional Control

Reduces stress and emotional strain associated with holding loose positions.

3. Techniques for Cutting Losses Early

a. Stop-Loss Orders

Definition: A stop-loss order is a pre-set order to sell a security when it reaches a certain price, limiting the trader's loss of a position.

Strategy:

Placement: Set stop-loss orders at strategic levels based on technical analysis, such as below support levels for long positions or above resistance levels for short positions.

Types: Use fixed stop-loss orders, trailing stops, or percentage-based stops.

b. Risk Management Rules

Definition: Establish rules that define the maximum amount of capital you're willing to risk on a single trade.

Strategy:

Risk Percentage: Limit each trade to a small percentage of your total capital, typically 1-2%.

Position Sizing: Calculate position size based on the distance between your entry point and stop-loss level.

4. Implementing a Cutting Losses Strategy

a. Develop a Trading Plan

Include detailed rules for stop-loss placement and risk management.

Ensure consistency in applying these rules across all trades.

b. Regular Review

Maintain a trading journal to track your trades and outcomes.

Review past trades to assess if stop-loss levels were effective and make necessary adjustments.

5. Psychological Considerations

a. Accepting Losses

Understand that losses are a natural part of trading.

Focus on the overall trading strategy and long-term profitability rather than individual losses.

b. Discipline and Patience

Stick to your trading plan and avoid moving stop-loss levels based on emotions.

Be patient and wait for high-probability setups before entering trades.

c. Confidence Building

Gain confidence in your trading plan through practice, back-testing, and education.

Regularly review and refine your strategy to ensure it remains effective.

Summary

Cutting your losses early is a fundamental aspect of successful trading. By implementing stop-loss orders, adhering to risk management rules, using technical analysis, and maintaining discipline, traders can effectively manage and minimize losses. Regular review and adaptation of your strategy ensure that it remains effective in various market conditions, ultimately contributing to long-term trading success.

5. RISK MANAGEMENT MISTAKES AND SOLUTIONS

Effective risk management is essential for long-term success in trading. However, many traders make common mistakes that can jeopardize their capital and trading career. Below are some common risk management mistakes and their corresponding solutions.

1. Ignoring Stop-Loss Orders

Mistake: Failing to use stop-loss orders can lead to substantial losses if the market moves against your position.

Solution:

Always Set Stop-Loss Orders: Define a stop-loss level for every trade to limit potential losses. Ensure the stop-loss is based on technical analysis, such as support and resistance levels.

Use Trailing Stops: Implement trailing stops to lock in profits while protecting against reversals.

2. Poor Position Sizing

Mistake: Inconsistent or overly large position sizes can result in significant losses.

Solution:

Determine Position Size Based on Risk: Calculate position size using a fixed percentage of your trading capital, such as risking only 1-2% per trade.

Use Position Sizing Formulas: Apply formulas that consider account equity, risk tolerance, and trade risk (difference between entry and stop-loss price).

3. Emotional Trading

Mistake: Allowing emotions such as fear, greed, or impatience to influence trading decisions often leads to poor outcomes.

Solution:

Follow a Trading Plan: Develop and adhere to a well-defined trading plan that outlines entry and exit criteria, risk management rules, and position sizing.

Practice Discipline: Stick to your plan and avoid impulsive decisions. Use automated trading systems or set alerts to help manage trades objectively.

4. Failing to Adapt to Market Conditions

Mistake: Using the same strategy regardless of changing market conditions can result in losses when market dynamics shift.

Solution:

Stay Informed: Continuously monitor market conditions and economic indicators that could impact your trades.

Adapt Strategies: Be flexible and adjust your trading strategies based on current market trends, volatility, and economic data.

5. Overtrading

Mistake: Taking too many trades, often due to the fear of missing out (FOMO), can lead to increased transaction costs and greater exposure to risk.

Solution:

Set Trade Limits: Define the maximum number of trades per day or week to avoid overtrading.

Quality Over Quantity: Focus on high-probability setups and avoid trading for the sake of activity.

6. Inadequate Risk-Reward Analysis

Mistake: Entering trades without assessing the potential risk versus reward can lead to poor risk management.

Solution:

Calculate Risk-Reward Ratios: Ensure each trade has a favourable risk-reward ratio (e.g., 1:2 or higher). Only take trades where the potential reward justifies the risk.

Stick to Your Criteria: Avoid taking trades that do not meet your predefined risk-reward criteria.

7. Ignoring Trade Review and Analysis

Mistake: Failing to review past trades can result in repeated mistakes and missed opportunities for improvement.

Solution:

Keep a Trading Journal: Document each trade, including the rationale, entry and exit points, and outcomes. Analyze the data to identify patterns and areas for improvement.

Regular Review: Periodically review your trading journal and performance metrics to refine your strategies and improve risk management practices.

8. Not Having a Contingency Plan

Mistake: Lack of a plan for unexpected events, such as sudden market crashes or platform failures, can lead to significant losses.

Solution:

Develop a Contingency Plan: Outline steps to take in the event of unexpected market events, technical issues, or personal emergencies.

Implement Safeguards: Use features like guaranteed stop-loss orders, backup internet connections, and alternative trading platforms.

By recognizing and addressing these common risk management mistakes, traders can enhance their strategies, protect their capital, and increase their chances of long-term success in the markets.

Chapter 4

Trading Psychology

Trading psychology is a critical aspect of successful trading. It involves understanding and managing the emotional and psychological factors that influence trading decisions.

1. FEAR OF MISSING OUT [FOMO]

Fear of missing out (FOMO) is a common psychological phenomenon in trading that can lead to impulsive and irrational decisions. It occurs when traders feel the urge to enter trades due to the fear that they might miss a significant opportunity, often driven by observing market movements or hearing about others' successes. Most of the traders made this mistake in their early trading days. The market is trading in a range for hours, not waiting for a breakout or breakdown before entry and losing money. Here are strategies to manage and overcome FOMO in trading:

1. Understanding FOMO in Trading

Emotional Trigger: Recognise that FOMO is an emotional response often triggered by seeing rapid market movements or hearing about others' profitable trades.

Impulsive Behaviour: FOMO can lead to impulsive decisions, such as chasing trends, entering trades without proper analysis, or overtrading.

2. Establish a Solid Trading Plan

Clear Criteria: Develop a detailed trading plan with specific criteria for entering and exiting trades. This helps you make decisions based on logic and analysis rather than emotions.

Stick to the Plan: Commit to following your trading plan strictly, regardless of market noise or external influences.

3. Mindfulness and Emotional Control

Stay Present: Practice mindfulness techniques to stay focused on the present moment and current market conditions rather than past missed opportunities or potential future gains.

Deep Breathing: Use deep breathing exercises to calm your mind and reduce anxiety before making trading decisions.

4. Discipline and Patience

Wait for Setups: Be patient and wait for high-probability trading setups that meet your predefined criteria. Avoid jumping into trades out of fear of missing out.

Avoid Overtrading: Recognise that not every market movement requires action. Sometimes, the best trade is no trade.

5. Educational and Community Support

Continuous Learning: Invest in your trading education by reading books, taking courses, and staying updated with market analysis to build confidence in your strategies.

Community Engagement: Join trading communities or find a mentor to share experiences and gain support. Discussing trades with others can provide different perspectives and reduce the feeling of missing out.

6. Technology and Automation

Automated Trading Systems: Consider using automated trading systems or algorithms that can execute trades based on predefined criteria, reducing the influence of emotions.

Alerts and Reminders: Set up alerts and reminders for potential trade setups, ensuring you don't miss opportunities without the pressure of constant market monitoring.

Practical Tips to Combat FOMO

Set Realistic Goals: Define realistic trading goals based on your capital, risk tolerance, and market conditions. This helps you stay grounded and reduces the pressure to chase every opportunity.

Recognise Market Cycles: Understand that markets go through cycles of uptrends, downtrends, and consolidations. Missing one opportunity does not mean there won't be others.

Focus on Process, Not Profits: Emphasise the importance of following your trading process and strategy rather than fixating on potential profits. This shift in focus can reduce the emotional impact of FOMO.

Embrace Missed Opportunities: Accept that missing out on trades is part of the trading experience. Use missed opportunities as learning experiences rather than sources of regret.

Limit Information Overload: Avoid consuming excessive market news or social media updates that can trigger FOMO. Focus on information that aligns with your trading plan and strategy.

Summary

Managing the fear of missing out in trading involves developing a disciplined approach, focusing on a solid trading plan, and maintaining emotional control. By understanding the triggers of FOMO and implementing strategies to mitigate its impact, traders can make more rational and informed decisions, leading to greater consistency and success in their trading endeavours.

2. TAKING RESPONSIBILITY

"Your life begins to change the day you take responsibility for it."

Taking responsibility in trading is a crucial aspect of developing into a successful trader. It involves acknowledging that you are accountable for your trading decisions, outcomes, and overall performance. Here are the key components of taking responsibility in trading:

Ownership of Decisions

Recognize that every trade you enter, hold, or exit is a result of your own decision-making process. Avoid blaming external factors such as the market, news, or others for your trading outcomes.

Embrace both successful and unsuccessful trades as learning opportunities driven by your own actions.

Learning from Mistakes

Analyze losing trades to identify what went wrong and how you can improve. Understand that mistakes are part of the learning process and provide valuable insights for future trades.

Develop a mindset that sees mistakes as opportunities for growth rather than reasons for frustration or self-blame.

Emotional Accountability

Take responsibility for your emotional responses to market movements. Recognise when emotions such as fear, greed, or frustration are influencing your trading decisions.

Develop techniques to manage emotions, such as mindfulness, meditation, or taking breaks during high-stress periods.

Consistent Discipline

Adhere to your trading plan and rules consistently. Taking responsibility means maintaining discipline even when it's challenging or when emotions are high.

Understand that discipline is key to long-term success and that deviating from your plan often leads to negative outcomes.

Accountability to Self

Hold yourself accountable for your trading performance. Set specific, measurable goals and track your progress towards achieving them.

If you experience setbacks or fail to meet your goals, evaluate your approach, and make necessary adjustments to improve.

Honest Self-Assessment

Conduct honest self-assessments of your trading performance regularly. Evaluate your strengths, weaknesses, and areas for improvement objectively.

Seek feedback from mentors, peers, or trading communities to gain different perspectives on your trading practices.

Ethical Trading Practices

Adhere to ethical standards in your trading activities. Ensure transparency, honesty, and integrity in your trading practices.

Taking responsibility also means considering the broader impact of your trading decisions on the market and other participants.

By taking full responsibility for your trading activities, you empower yourself to make better decisions, learn from your experiences, and continuously improve your trading skills. This approach fosters a sense of control and ownership, leading to more disciplined and successful trading over the long-term.

3. REVENGE TRADING

"When you begin a journey of revenge, start by digging 2 graves: one for your enemy and one for yourself"

– Jodi Picoult

Revenge trading occurs when a trader attempts to recover losses from previous trades by taking impulsive and excessive risks. This behaviour is driven by emotions such as frustration, anger, or a desire to "get back" at the market. However, revenge trading often leads to further losses and exacerbates the trader's emotional distress. Here are some strategies to help traders avoid revenge trading:

1. Acknowledge and Accept Emotions

Self-Awareness: Recognise when you're experiencing emotions such as frustration, anger, or disappointment after a losing trade. Acknowledge these feelings without acting on them impulsively.

Acceptance: Accept that losses are a natural part of trading and that no trader is immune to them. Understand that revenge trading is a reaction to emotional pain and is not a rational solution.

2. Take a Break

Cooling-Off Period: Step away from the trading screen and take a break to calm down and regain perspective. Engage in activities that help you relax and decompress, such as exercise, meditation, or spending time with loved ones.

Time-Out: Give yourself time to reflect on the reasons behind your losses and identify any patterns or mistakes in your trading approach. Use this time for self-reflection and learning rather than rushing back into trading.

3. Stick to Your Trading Plan

Discipline: Remind yourself of the importance of sticking to your trading plan and following your predefined risk management rules. Avoid deviating from your plan out of a desire for revenge or to recoup losses quickly.

Focus on Process: Shift your focus from trying to recover losses to executing your trading strategy effectively. Emphasise disciplined and patient trading rather than chasing profits.

4. Protect your Capital

Protect Your Capital: Prioritise capital preservation by implementing proper risk management.

Techniques, such as setting stop-loss orders and controlling position sizes. Avoid risking more than you can afford to lose in an attempt to recover losses.

Accept Small Losses: Accept that some losses are inevitable in trading and are part of the cost of doing business. Focus on managing risk and minimising the impact of losses rather than avoiding them altogether.

5. Continuous Learning

Learn from Mistakes: Use losing trades as learning opportunities to identify areas for improvement in your trading strategy, risk management, or emotional discipline.

Educate Yourself: Invest in your trading education by learning about trading psychology, risk management, and strategies for overcoming emotional biases. The more you understand about trading, the better equipped you'll be to handle losses effectively.

6. Seek Support and Accountability

Trading Community: Surround yourself with a supportive network of fellow traders, mentors, or trading communities who can offer guidance, perspective, and encouragement during challenging times.

Accountability Partner: Partner with a trading buddy or mentor who can hold you accountable for your trading plan and help you stay disciplined. Share your experiences and challenges with them openly.

7. Set Realistic Expectations

Long-Term Perspective: Remember that trading success is measured over the long-term, not by individual trades. Avoid placing unrealistic expectations on yourself or expecting to win every trade.

Focus on Consistency: Aim for consistency and steady progress in your trading rather than trying to make up for losses with big wins. Small, consistent gains can add up over time and contribute to long-term success.

Summary

Revenge trading can have serious consequences for traders, including further losses, emotional distress, and damage to confidence. By acknowledging and accepting emotions, taking breaks to regain perspective, sticking to their trading plan, practising risk management, continuous learning, seeking support, and setting realistic expectations, traders can avoid falling into the trap of revenge trading and maintain a disciplined and rational approach to their trading

4. DON'T CHASE THE PRICE

Chasing the price in trading refers to entering trades at unfavourable prices due to impulsive or emotional reactions to market movements. This behaviour often leads to poor trading decisions and increased risk of losses. Here are some reasons why traders should avoid chasing the price and strategies to prevent it:

Reasons to Avoid Chasing the Price

Increased Risk: Chasing the price often leads to entering trades at less favourable levels, increasing the risk of losses if the market reverses.

Emotional Decision-Making: Chasing trades is usually driven by emotions such as fear of missing out (FOMO) or greed rather than rational analysis.

Poor Risk-Reward Ratio: Trades entered after chasing the price may have a less favourable risk-reward ratio, potentially resulting in larger losses relative to potential gains.

Undermines Trading Plan: Chasing trades deviates from a trader's predetermined trading plan and criteria, leading to inconsistent and undisciplined trading.

Strategies to Avoid Chasing the Price

Patience and Discipline: Wait for trades that meet your predefined criteria and entry signals. Avoid entering trades impulsively based on short-term price movements.

Set Entry and Exit Points: Determine specific entry and exit points for your trades in advance. Stick to these levels regardless of short-term market fluctuations.

Use Limit Orders: Place limit orders at predetermined price levels to enter trades. This helps avoid chasing the price and ensures you enter trades at desired levels.

Focus on Quality Setups: Prioritise high-probability trade setups that align with your trading strategy and have clear reasons for entry.

Stay Informed, Not Reactive: Keep yourself informed about market developments and news, but avoid reacting impulsively to every price movement. Maintain a calm and rational mindset.

Summary

Chasing the price in trading is a common mistake that can lead to poor outcomes and increased risk. By practising patience, discipline, and proper risk management, traders can avoid chasing trades and focus on executing their trading plans with consistency and precision. This approach helps maintain a rational and objective mindset, leading to more successful and sustainable trading results over time.

5. PROBABILITY MINDSET

Trading is a probability game because the trade outcomes are variable in an uncertain market.

Adopting a probability mindset in trading is essential for managing risk, making informed decisions, and achieving long-term success. This mindset involves viewing each trade as a probabilistic event rather than a guaranteed outcome, focusing on the overall performance of a trading strategy rather than individual trades. Here are key aspects and strategies to develop and maintain a probability mindset in trading:

1. Understanding Probabilities in Trading

Probabilistic Nature of Markets: Acknowledge that markets are influenced by countless factors, making outcomes inherently uncertain and probabilistic.

Expected Value: Focus on the expected value of trades, which is the average outcome of a trading strategy over many trades, taking into account both wins and losses.

2. Trade Setup and Entry Criteria

High-Probability Setups: Identify and trade setups that have a higher probability of success based on historical data, patterns, and technical indicators.

Clear Entry and Exit Criteria: Define specific criteria for entering and exiting trades to ensure decisions are based on strategy rather than emotions.

3. Detach from Outcomes

Understand that each trade is just one instance within a larger series of trades. Don't get emotionally attached to individual outcomes.

Stay Consistent: Stick to your trading plan and strategy even after a series of wins or losses. Consistency is key to leveraging the probability mindset.

4. Analysing Trade Performance

Trading Journal: Keep a detailed trading journal documenting each trade, including entry and exit points, rationale, emotions, and outcomes. This helps analyse patterns and improve strategies.

Review and Reflect: Regularly review your trading journal to identify what works and what doesn't, focusing on the probability of different setups and strategies.

5. Back-testing and Forward Testing

Historical Data: Back-test your trading strategies using historical data to understand their performance over various market conditions and identify their probability of success.

Demo Trading: Use demo accounts or paper trading to forward test strategies in real-time without risking actual capital.

Practical Steps to Develop a Probability Mindset

Calculate Risk-Reward Ratio

For each trade, determine the potential risk (the amount you could lose) versus the potential reward (the amount you could gain). A favourable risk-reward ratio (e.g., 1:2) ensures that even with a lower win rate, you can be profitable over time.

Use Probabilistic Language

Think and speak in terms of probabilities. Instead of saying, "This trade will make money," say, "This trade has a 60% probability of being profitable."

Scenario Planning

Develop multiple scenarios for each trade, including best-case, worst-case, and most likely.

Outcomes. This helps in understanding the range of possible results and preparing for different market conditions.

Mindfulness and Stress Reduction

Practice mindfulness techniques to stay calm and focused. Stress reduction strategies such as meditation, exercise, and proper rest are crucial for maintaining a clear and disciplined mindset.

Celebrate Process, Not Outcomes

Celebrate adherence to your trading process and strategy rather than the outcome of individual trades. This reinforces good habits and maintains a probability-focused approach.

Summary

A probability mindset in trading emphasizes the importance of viewing trades as part of a larger statistical framework rather than isolated events. By focusing on risk management, consistency, and continuous improvement, traders can better navigate the inherent uncertainties of the market. This approach not only enhances decision-making and emotional control but also increases the likelihood of long-term success in trading.

6. BONDING WITH THE MONEY

Bonding with money in trading refers to developing an emotional attachment or fixation on the profits or losses generated from trading activities. From childhood, we learned from our parents that money is very important. If trade goes against our direction, novice traders may panic. This emotional attachment can lead to irrational decision-making, increased stress, and poor trading outcomes. Here are some reasons why bonding with money in trading can be detrimental and strategies to overcome it:

Reasons Why Bonding with Money in Trading is Detrimental

Emotional Decision-Making: Bonding with money can cloud judgement and lead to emotionally driven trading decisions, such as holding onto losing trades for too long or exiting winning trades prematurely.

Fear and Anxiety: The fear of losing money can cause anxiety and stress, impairing a trader's ability to make rational decisions and stick to their trading plan.

Overtrading: Traders may engage in excessive trading in an attempt to recoup losses or capitalise on winning streaks, leading to increased transaction costs and higher risk exposure.

Loss Aversion: Traders may become overly risk-averse, avoiding potentially profitable opportunities out of fear of losing money, thereby limiting their trading potential.

Attachment to Outcomes: Bonding with money can lead to an unhealthy attachment to trading outcomes, causing emotional distress, and impacting overall well-being.

Strategies to Overcome Bonding with Money in Trading

Focus on Process, Not Outcome: Shift your focus from the monetary outcome of individual trades to the process of executing your trading plan effectively. Emphasise disciplined and rational decision-making. When trades are going on, focusing on charts rather than money is important.

Acceptance of Uncertainty: Acknowledge that trading involves inherent uncertainty and that losses are a natural part of the process. Embrace uncertainty and focus on managing risk rather than avoiding losses.

Set Realistic Goals: Establish realistic and achievable trading goals that are based on factors within your control, such as following your trading plan and managing risk effectively.

Practice Mindfulness: Cultivate mindfulness techniques, such as meditation or deep breathing exercises, to stay present and calm during trading sessions. Be aware of your emotions and thoughts without becoming attached to them.

Detach from Outcomes: Detach your self-worth and identity from trading outcomes. Recognise that your value as a person is not determined by your success or failure as a trader.

Develop a Long-Term Perspective: Adopt a long-term view of trading success and focus on building sustainable wealth over time rather than chasing short-term gains.

Diversify Income Streams: Explore alternative sources of income outside of trading to reduce financial dependence on trading profits. Diversification can help alleviate the pressure and emotional attachment associated with trading.

Summary

Bonding with money in trading can lead to detrimental trading behaviours and emotional distress. By shifting the focus from monetary outcomes to the trading process, accepting uncertainty, setting realistic goals, practising mindfulness, detaching from outcomes, maintaining a long-term perspective, diversifying income streams, and seeking professional help if needed, traders can overcome emotional attachment to money and make more rational and disciplined trading decisions. This approach can lead to improved trading outcomes and overall well-being in the long run.

7. MARKET IS ALWAYS RIGHT

The phrase "the market is always right" encapsulates a fundamental principle in trading: markets are driven by the collective actions and sentiments of all participants, and their price movements reflect the aggregate information, beliefs, and emotions at any given time. Embracing this concept can help traders adopt a more humble, disciplined, and adaptive approach. Here are key insights and strategies related to this principle:

Key Insights

Price Reflects All Information: Market prices incorporate all known information, including economic data, news, and investor sentiment. Accepting this helps traders avoid the trap of fighting against the market trend.

Market Trends and Sentiments: Trends and market sentiment often drive price movements more than fundamental factors. Understanding and aligning with market sentiment is crucial for successful trading.

Avoiding Bias: Believing that the market is always right helps traders avoid cognitive biases, such as confirmation bias, where they might only seek information that supports their preconceived notions.

Strategies to Embrace the Principle

Follow the Trend: Rather than trying to predict market reversals, follow established trends. The adage "the trend is your friend" underscores the importance of aligning your trades with prevailing market directions.

Stay Informed, Not Predictive: Keep abreast of market news and data, but avoid making trades based on predictions. Instead, respond to what the market is currently doing.

Implement Strong Risk Management: Use stop-loss and take-profit orders to manage risk. Acknowledge that any trade can go against you and plan accordingly to protect your capital.

Embrace Flexibility and Adaptability: Be willing to change your trading strategy if the market conditions change. Rigidity and stubbornness can lead to significant losses.

Learn from Mistakes: Review your trades regularly to learn from both your successes and failures. Understand why certain trades did not work out and adjust your strategy to align better with market realities.

Maintain Emotional Discipline: Keep emotions in check. Fear and greed can cloud judgement. Developing emotional discipline helps you stick to your trading plan and avoid impulsive decisions.

Conclusion

Accepting that "the market is always right" is a mindset that fosters humility, discipline, and adaptability in trading. By aligning with market trends, utilising technical analysis, managing risk effectively, staying informed without being predictive, embracing flexibility, learning from past trades, and maintaining emotional discipline, traders can improve their chances of success. This approach acknowledges the collective wisdom of the market and helps traders navigate the complexities of trading with a clearer, more objective perspective.

8. TAKING PROFITS

Taking profits in trading is a crucial aspect of risk management and overall trading strategy. It involves deciding when to close a profitable position to maximise gains while minimising the risk of giving back profits. Always watching the profits are not yours; lock the profits only yours. Here are some strategies and considerations for effectively taking profits:

1. Set Profit Targets

Predefined Targets: Establish clear profit targets before entering a trade. These targets should be based on technical analysis, such as resistance levels, Fibonacci retracements, or moving averages.

Risk-Reward Ratio: Determine your risk-reward ratio (e.g., 1:2 or 1:3) and set your profit targets accordingly. For instance, if you risk Rs 100, aim to make at least Rs 200 or Rs 300 to maintain a favourable risk-reward ratio.

2. Trailing Stops

Trailing Stop Orders: Use trailing stop orders to lock in profits as the market moves in your favour. A trailing stop automatically adjusts to price movements, allowing you to capture more profit while protecting against reversals.

Manual Adjustment: Alternatively, manually adjust your stop-loss order to a breakeven point or above once the trade is in profit. This ensures you don't lose capital while giving the trade room to move.

3. Partial Profit-Taking

Scale-Out: Take partial profits at predetermined levels. For example, close half of your position at the first target and let the remainder run to the next target. This strategy balances securing gains with the potential for further upside.

Lock in Gains: Scaling out allows you to lock in gains and reduce risk while still participating in the trade if the market continues to move in your favour.

4. Technical Indicators

Momentum Indicators: Use momentum indicators such as RSI (Relative Strength Index) or MACD (Moving Average Convergence Divergence) to identify overbought conditions and potential reversal points where taking profits might be wise.

Price Action: Pay attention to price action signals such as candlestick patterns, trendlines, CPR and support/resistance levels to determine when to exit a trade.

5. Market Conditions

Volatility: Adjust your profit-taking strategy based on market volatility. In highly volatile markets, consider tighter profit targets to capture quick gains. In trending markets, allow your trades more room to run.

Economic Events: Be aware of upcoming economic events or news releases that could impact the market. Consider taking profits ahead of such events to avoid potential adverse price movements.

6. Psychological Discipline

Stick to Your Plan: Follow your trading plan and resist the temptation to alter your profit targets based on emotions. Emotional decisions can lead to premature exits or holding onto trades too long.

Greed Management: Avoid the trap of holding onto winning trades indefinitely out of greed. It's better to take consistent, smaller profits than to risk losing gains by waiting for unrealistic price moves.

7. Review and Adapt

Performance Analysis: Regularly review your trading performance to identify patterns in your profit-taking decisions. Learn from both your successes and mistakes to refine your strategy.

Adapt Strategy: Be flexible and willing to adjust your profit-taking strategy based on market conditions, your trading style, and your evolving understanding of the markets.

Summary

Effectively taking profits in trading involves a combination of predefined targets, technical analysis, risk management techniques, and psychological discipline. By setting clear profit targets, using trailing stops, scaling out of positions, relying on technical indicators, considering market conditions, maintaining psychological discipline, and continuously reviewing and adapting your approach, you can enhance your ability to capture gains while protecting your capital. This disciplined approach to profit-taking can contribute significantly to long-term trading success.

9. LIMITING BELIEFS IN TRADING

Limiting beliefs in trading can hinder a trader's success by creating mental barriers that prevent them from reaching their full potential. These beliefs can manifest in various forms, such as self-doubt, fear of failure, or rigid thinking patterns. Here are some common limiting beliefs in trading and strategies to overcome them:

1. Fear of Failure

Limiting Belief: "I'm afraid of losing money in the markets."

Solution:

Risk Management: Implement robust risk management techniques, such as position sizing and stop-loss orders, to limit potential losses.

Mindfulness: Practice mindfulness techniques to stay present and focused on the process rather than dwelling on potential failures.

Positive Affirmations: Repeat affirmations that reinforce confidence and resilience, such as "I am a disciplined and successful trader."

2. Perfectionism

Limiting Belief: "I must always make perfect trades to be successful."

Solution:

Acceptance of Imperfection: Understand that losses and mistakes are inevitable in trading. Focus on learning from failures and improving over time.

Flexibility: Be adaptable and willing to adjust your strategies based on changing market conditions rather than seeking perfection.

Focus on Progress: Measure success not by achieving perfection in every trade but by making progress toward your long-term trading goals.

3. Self-Doubt

Limiting Belief: "I'm not good enough to be a successful trader."

Solution:

Positive Self-Talk: Challenge negative self-talk by replacing it with positive affirmations and reminders of past successes.

Visualisation: Visualise yourself executing successful trades and achieving your trading goals to build confidence and self-belief.

Seek Support: Surround yourself with supportive peers, mentors, or trading communities who can provide encouragement and constructive feedback.

4. Fear of Missing Out (FOMO)

Limiting Belief: "I must enter every trade to avoid missing out on opportunities."

Solution:

Discipline: Stick to your trading plan and only enter trades that meet your predefined criteria. Accept that missed opportunities are part of trading.

Focus on Quality: Prioritise high-probability setups over chasing every market movement. Quality trades are more important than quantity.

Mindfulness: Stay present and focused on the current trade rather than worrying about potential missed opportunities.

5. Rigid Thinking

Limiting Belief: "There's only one right way to trade, and I must follow it."

Solution:

Open-Mindedness: Be open to exploring different trading strategies, techniques, and perspectives. What works for one trader may not work for another.

Continuous Learning: Embrace a growth mindset and commit to ongoing education and self-improvement. Experiment with new ideas and adapt your approach based on feedback and results.

Reflective Practice: Regularly review your trading performance and decisions to identify areas for improvement and opportunities for growth.

6. Overemphasis on Past Mistakes

Limiting Belief: "I made a bad trade in the past, so I'll probably make the same mistake again."

Solution:

Learn from Mistakes: Analyse past mistakes to understand what went wrong and identify areas for improvement. Use this knowledge to make better decisions in the future.

Focus on the Present: Stay focused on the current trade rather than dwelling on past failures. Each trade is an opportunity to apply what you've learned and improve your performance.

Forgive Yourself: Practice self-compassion and forgive yourself for past mistakes. Everyone makes errors, but what matters is how you learn and grow from them.

7. External Locus of Control

Limiting Belief: "I can't succeed in trading because the markets are manipulated/out of my control."

Solution:

Internal Locus of Control: Focus on factors within your control, such as your trading strategy, risk management, and emotional discipline. Accept that while you can't control market movements, you can control how you react to them.

Adaptability: Be adaptable and responsive to changing market conditions rather than feeling helpless in the face of uncertainty.

Empowerment: Take ownership of your trading journey and actively seek ways to improve your skills and knowledge. Believe in your ability to succeed through your efforts and determination.

Summary

Overcoming limiting beliefs in trading requires a combination of self-awareness, emotional resilience, and proactive strategies. By identifying and challenging these beliefs, traders can cultivate a positive mindset and develop the confidence and adaptability needed to achieve success in the markets.

Chapter 5

Trading Mindset

1. WHY I AM TRADING

INTRODUCTION

Understanding why you are trading is crucial for defining your goals, developing a suitable strategy, and maintaining motivation and discipline. Here are some common reasons why people trade, along with the implications of each motivation:

Common Reasons for Trading

Financial Independence

Goal: Achieve financial freedom and independence by generating income through trading.

Implications: Requires a solid understanding of the markets, consistent profitability, and disciplined risk management to replace or supplement regular income.

Wealth Building

Goal: Build long-term wealth by growing your trading account over time.

Implications: Focus on strategies that compound returns and emphasize capital preservation. Requires patience and a long-term perspective.

Income Generation

Goal: Generate a regular income stream from trading activities.

Implications: Requires strategies that provide consistent returns and manage risk effectively to ensure a steady income.

Passion for Markets

Goal: Engage in trading out of a passion for financial markets and the intellectual challenge they provide.

Implications: Maintaining enthusiasm can lead to continuous learning and improvement, but it's essential to balance passion with discipline.

Lifestyle Flexibility

Goal: Attain a flexible lifestyle that allows for trading from anywhere and at any time.

Implications: Requires mastery of trading strategies that can be managed remotely and the ability to maintain discipline outside a structured environment.

Supplemental Income

Goal: Earn additional income alongside other primary sources of income (e.g., a job or business).

Implications: Focus on strategies that do not require constant monitoring and allow for part-time involvement in trading.

Reflection Questions to Clarify Your Motivation

What Are My Financial Goals?

Determine whether you aim for short-term income, long-term wealth, or financial independence. This will guide your choice of trading strategies and time horizons.

How Much Risk Am I Willing to Take?

Assess your risk tolerance to ensure your trading activities align with your comfort level and financial situation.

What Is My Time Commitment?

Evaluate how much time you can realistically dedicate to trading. This will help you choose between day trading, swing trading, or longer-term investing.

What Is My Level of Experience?

Consider your current knowledge and experience in trading. Beginners might focus on learning and small-scale trades, while experienced traders might employ more sophisticated strategies.

What Resources Do I Have?

Assess your financial resources, technology, and access to information. Ensure you have the necessary tools and capital to support your trading activities.

What Are My Strengths and Weaknesses?

Reflect on your personal attributes, such as analytical skills, emotional control, and discipline. This self-awareness can help tailor your trading approach to suit your strengths.

Summary

Understanding why you are trading is a foundational step that shapes every aspect of your trading journey, from goal setting and strategy development to risk management and emotional discipline. By reflecting on your motivations, you can align your trading activities with your personal and financial goals, ensuring a more focused, disciplined, and ultimately successful approach to the markets.

2. TRADING IS A BUSINESS

Viewing trading as a business is a fundamental mindset shift that can lead to more disciplined, systematic, and sustainable trading practices. Here's how treating trading as a business can benefit traders.

Benefits of Treating Trading as a Business

Professionalism: Adopting a business mindset encourages traders to approach their activities with professionalism, discipline, and a long-term perspective.

Systematic Approach: Trading like a business involves developing and following a systematic trading plan with clear objectives, strategies, and risk management rules.

Risk Management: Emphasizing risk management is essential in a business approach to trading. Traders prioritize capital preservation and focus on managing risk effectively to protect their investment.

Continuous Improvement: Treating trading as a business encourages ongoing learning, self-improvement, and adaptation to market conditions. Traders seek to refine their skills, strategies, and processes over time.

Accountability: Traders take responsibility for their actions and decisions, holding themselves accountable for their performance and results.

Summary

Treating trading as a business entails adopting a professional, disciplined, and systematic approach to trading. By developing a comprehensive trading plan, emphasising risk management, conducting thorough market analysis, executing trades with discipline, continuously learning, and improving, and regularly reviewing performance, traders can enhance their profitability, consistency, and long-term success in the financial markets. Remember that trading is a business endeavour that requires dedication, diligence, and ongoing commitment to excellence.

3. TRADING IN THE MOMENT

Trading in the moment, often referred to as "being in the zone" or "trading in the flow," involves making trading decisions based on the current market conditions without being influenced by past trades or future expectations. It requires a high level of focus, discipline, and the ability to adapt quickly to changing market dynamics. Here are some key principles and strategies for effectively trading at the moment:

1. Mindfulness and Focus

Stay Present: Focus on the present moment and current market conditions rather than dwelling on past trades or worrying about future outcomes.

Mindfulness Practices: Engage in mindfulness exercises, such as meditation or deep breathing, to enhance your ability to stay present and calm.

2. Preparation and Planning

Pre-Market Routine: Develop a pre-market routine to prepare mentally and strategically for the trading day. This can include reviewing news, analyzing charts, and setting key levels.

Clear Strategy: Have a well-defined trading strategy and plan, including entry and exit criteria, risk management rules, and contingency plans.

3. Emotional Discipline

Control Emotions: Recognize and manage emotions such as fear, greed, and overconfidence. Emotional discipline helps prevent impulsive decisions that can lead to losses.

Detach from Outcomes: Focus on executing your trading plan rather than being emotionally attached to the results of individual trades.

4. Adaptability and Flexibility

Read the Market: Continuously read and interpret market signals and price action. Be prepared to adjust your strategy based on real-time information.

Be Flexible: Adapt to changing market conditions by being flexible in your approach. This might involve switching between different trading strategies or adjusting your risk management tactics.

5. Continuous Learning and Improvement

Review and Reflect: After trading sessions, review your trades to understand what worked and what didn't. Reflect on your decision-making process and emotional state during trades.

Seek Feedback: Engage with other traders, mentors, or trading communities to gain insights and feedback on your trading approach.

Practical Tips for Trading in the Moment

Create a Distraction-Free Environment: Ensure your trading environment is free from distractions. A calm and focused setting helps you concentrate fully on the market.

Develop a Trading Journal: Maintain a trading journal to record your trades, including the rationale behind each trade, the emotions you experienced, and the outcome. This helps identify patterns and areas for improvement.

Set Realistic Goals: Set achievable trading goals based on your experience and market conditions. Realistic goals keep you motivated and focused without undue pressure.

Regular Breaks and Self-Care: Take regular breaks to avoid burnout and maintain mental clarity. Self-care practices, such as exercise, proper nutrition, and adequate sleep, are crucial for sustained performance.

Summary

Trading at the moment involves a combination of mindfulness, preparation, emotional discipline, and adaptability. By focusing on the present and making decisions based on current market conditions, traders can improve their performance and achieve greater consistency. Implementing these strategies helps traders stay in the zone, react appropriately to market movements, and maintain a balanced and objective approach to trading.

4. CAREFREE STATE OF MIND

Achieving a carefree state of mind in trading is about developing a psychological state where you can trade without being emotionally affected by the outcomes of individual trades. This state allows you to execute your trading plan with discipline and objectivity, free from the fear of loss or the pressure to perform. Here are some strategies to cultivate a carefree state of mind in trading:

1. Develop a Solid Trading Plan

Clear Strategy: Have a well-defined trading strategy that includes entry and exit criteria, risk management rules, and position sizing. Knowing you have a plan helps reduce uncertainty and stress.

Consistency: Stick to your trading plan regardless of short-term outcomes. Consistency in following your strategy builds confidence and reduces emotional volatility.

2. Financial Security

Trade with Disposable Income: Ensure that the capital you are trading with is money you can afford to lose. This reduces the financial pressure and allows you to trade more freely.

Diversification: Diversify your investments to spread risk. Knowing that your financial well-being does not depend on a single trade or market reduces stress.

Practical Tips for a Carefree State of Mind

Set Realistic Expectations

Understand that trading is not a get-rich-quick scheme. Setting realistic goals and expectations reduces pressure and disappointment.

Limit Screen Time

Avoid constantly monitoring the markets and your trades. Set specific times to check your trades, which helps prevent emotional reactions to market fluctuations.

Take Breaks

Take regular breaks to refresh your mind and prevent burnout. Stepping away from the screen can provide perspective and reduce stress.

Celebrate Small Wins

Acknowledge and celebrate small victories and milestones. Positive reinforcement helps maintain motivation and a positive mindset.

Develop Hobbies and Interests

Engage in activities outside of trading that you enjoy and that help you relax. A well-rounded life reduces the emotional intensity of trading.

Summary

Cultivating a carefree state of mind in trading is about balancing discipline, emotional control, and a healthy perspective on the role of trading in your life. By focusing on the process, managing risk effectively, and maintaining emotional discipline, you can trade with greater confidence and less emotional stress. This approach not only enhances your trading performance but also contributes to a healthier and more enjoyable trading experience.

5. IMPROVING TRADING PSYCHOLOGY

Improving trading psychology is essential for success in the markets. Here are some solutions to help traders enhance their psychological resilience and emotional discipline:

1. Self-awareness and Emotional Regulation

Mindfulness Practices: Engage in mindfulness meditation, deep breathing exercises, or visualization techniques to increase self-awareness and regulate emotions.

Journaling: Keep a trading journal to track your thoughts, emotions, and behaviours during trades. Reviewing your journal regularly can help you identify patterns and triggers.

Identify Cognitive Biases: Learn about common cognitive biases that affect decision-making in trading, such as confirmation bias or loss aversion. Recognizing these biases can help you mitigate their impact.

2. Developing Discipline and Patience

Stick to Your Trading Plan: Create a detailed trading plan with predefined entry and exit criteria, risk management rules, and goals. Discipline yourself to follow this plan consistently.

Practice Delayed Gratification: Cultivate patience by focusing on the long-term outcomes of your trading decisions rather than seeking immediate gratification.

Set Realistic Expectations: Understand that trading success takes time and effort. Avoid expecting overnight results, and be prepared to face setbacks along the way.

3. Coping with Fear and Greed

Fear Management: Identify the sources of fear in your trading, whether it's fear of failure, fear of missing out, or fear of uncertainty. Develop strategies to address these fears, such as gradual exposure or reframing negative thoughts.

Greed Management: Recognize the dangers of greed and overconfidence in trading. Stay humble and disciplined, and avoid chasing unrealistic gains or taking excessive risks.

Stay Educated: Keep learning about trading psychology, market dynamics, and risk management strategies. Stay updated with market news and developments to adapt your approach accordingly.

Seek Feedback: Seek feedback from mentors, trading communities, or peers to gain different perspectives on your trading performance. Use constructive criticism to improve your skills and mindset.

4. Healthy Lifestyle Habits

Physical Exercise: Engage in regular physical activity to reduce stress, improve focus, and boost overall well-being.

Proper Nutrition and Sleep: Maintain a balanced diet and ensure adequate sleep to support cognitive function and emotional stability.

Social Support: Surround yourself with supportive friends, family members, or trading peers who understand the challenges of trading and can provide encouragement and advice.

5. Visualization and Positive Affirmations

Visualization: Visualize yourself executing successful trades and achieving your trading goals. Use imagery to reinforce positive behaviours and outcomes.

Positive Self-Talk: Replace negative self-talk with positive affirmations and reminders of your strengths and capabilities as a trader. Build confidence in your abilities to overcome challenges and achieve success.

Summary

Improving trading psychology requires a combination of self-awareness, emotional regulation, discipline, and continuous learning. By implementing these solutions and actively working on developing a resilient mindset, traders can enhance their ability to navigate the challenges of trading and achieve long-term success in the markets.

6. WINNING ATTITUDE

Developing a winning attitude in trading involves cultivating a mindset characterized by confidence, discipline, resilience, and a focus on continuous improvement. Always start with a small quantity and build your confidence. Here are some key elements and strategies to foster a winning attitude:

1. Positive Mindset

Belief in Success: Cultivate a belief in your ability to succeed as a trader. Trust in your skills, knowledge, and experience to achieve your trading goals.

Optimism: Maintain a positive outlook, even in the face of setbacks or challenges. View obstacles as opportunities for growth and learning.

Gratitude: Practice gratitude for the opportunities and resources available to you as a trader. Focus on what you have rather than what you lack.

2. Discipline and Consistency

Stick to Your Plan: Develop and adhere to a well-defined trading plan with clear entry and exit criteria, risk management rules, and goals.

Consistent Execution: Execute your trading plan with discipline and consistency, regardless of market conditions or emotions.

Resilience: Bounce back from losses or setbacks with resilience and determination. Learn from failures and use them as fuel for improvement.

3. Continuous Learning

Curiosity: aintain a curious and open-minded approach to learning. Stay updated with market developments, trading strategies, and psychological techniques.

Feedback: Seek feedback from mentors, trading communities, or peers to gain different perspectives on your trading performance. Use constructive criticism to improve your skills.

Adaptability: Be willing to adapt and evolve your trading approach based on new information, market conditions, and personal experiences.

4. Emotional Intelligence

Self-Awareness: Develop self-awareness of your emotions, thoughts, and behaviours while trading. Recognize and manage emotional triggers such as fear, greed, or overconfidence.

Emotional Regulation: Practice techniques such as deep breathing, visualisation, or mindfulness to regulate emotions and maintain a calm and focused state of mind.

Empathy: Develop empathy towards yourself and others. Treat yourself with compassion and understanding, especially during challenging times.

5. Goal Setting and Visualization

Clear Goals: Set specific, measurable, achievable, relevant, and time-bound (SMART) goals for your trading. Break down larger goals into smaller milestones to track progress.

Visualization: Visualize yourself achieving your trading goals with clarity and detail. Use imagery to reinforce positive behaviours, outcomes, and emotions associated with success.

Motivation: Use your goals and visualization techniques as sources of motivation and inspiration to stay committed to your trading journey.

6. Healthy Habits and Self-Care

Physical Health: Prioritize your physical well-being through regular exercise, proper nutrition, and sufficient sleep. Physical health directly impacts cognitive function and emotional resilience.

Mental Health Take care of your mental health by managing stress, practising relaxation techniques, and seeking professional support if needed.

Work-Life Balance: Maintain a healthy balance between your trading activities and other aspects of your life. Nurture relationships, pursue hobbies, and engage in activities that bring you joy and fulfilment outside of trading.

Summary

A winning attitude in trading is characterized by a positive mindset, discipline, continuous learning, emotional intelligence, goal setting, visualization, and self-care. By cultivating these qualities and implementing the strategies outlined above, traders can increase their chances of success and achieve their trading goals in the dynamic and challenging world of financial markets.

7. LESS TRADE MORE PROFIT

The statement "less trade, more profit; more trade highlights the importance of quality over quantity in trading. Monthly 40 to 50 trades are enough to make bigger money from the stock market." Here's an explanation, along with strategies to optimize trading frequency for greater profitability:

Less Trade, More Profit

Quality over Quantity: Focus on high-quality trade setups with strong technical or fundamental indications. Daily 2 or a maximum of 3 trades are more than enough to make consistent money in day trading. If anyone day no trade day is a good day. Prioritize trades that offer a favourable risk-reward ratio and align closely with your trading strategy.

Patience and Discipline: Exercise patience and discipline in waiting for optimal trade opportunities. Avoid overtrading and entering trades impulsively based on fear of missing out (FOMO) or boredom.

Selective Trading: Be selective in the trades you take, focusing on setups that have a high-probability of success and meet your predefined criteria. Avoid trading in choppy or uncertain market conditions.

Establish Clear Criteria: Define clear entry and exit criteria in your trading plan. Only take trades that meet these criteria, regardless of how frequently they occur.

Simulated Trading: Practice simulated trading or back-testing to test different trading frequencies and strategies. Determine which approach yields the best results and implement it in live trading with proper risk management.

Summary

Finding the right balance between trading frequency and profitability is essential for success in trading. By prioritizing quality over quantity, exercising patience and discipline, and implementing, you can optimize your trading frequency to maximize profitability while minimizing unnecessary risks and emotional stress. Remember that consistency and adherence to your trading plan are key to long-term success in trading.

8. BE PATIENCE IN TRADING

"The 2 most powerful warriors are patience and time"

– Leo Tolstoy

Practising patience in trading is essential for long-term success and emotional well-being. On the riverside, a crane sits for a few hours to catch a fish. In trading, we also have to wait for a few hours for proper entry level. Here are some reasons why patience is crucial in trading, along with strategies to cultivate and maintain it:

Importance of Patience in Trading

Waiting for Quality Setups: Patience allows traders to wait for high-probability trade setups that align with their trading strategy and have a favourable risk-reward ratio.

Avoiding Impulsive Decisions: Patience helps traders avoid making impulsive trading decisions based on emotions such as fear, greed, or boredom.

Maintaining Discipline: Patience enables traders to stick to their trading plan and follow their predefined entry and exit criteria, even during periods of market volatility or uncertainty.

Managing Expectations: Patience helps traders maintain realistic expectations and understand that trading success takes time, practice, and continuous learning.

Strategies to Cultivate Patience in Trading

Develop a Trading Plan: Create a well-defined trading plan with clear entry and exit criteria, risk management rules, and goals. Stick to your plan and avoid deviating from it due to impatience or emotional impulses.

Practice Delayed Gratification: Train yourself to delay immediate rewards for long-term gains. Understand that patience in trading often leads to better outcomes over time.

Set Realistic Goals: Establish achievable short-term and long-term goals for your trading. Break down larger goals into smaller milestones and celebrate your progress along the way.

Mindfulness and Meditation: Practice mindfulness techniques such as meditation, deep breathing, or visualisation to cultivate patience and stay present in the moment. Learn to observe your thoughts and emotions without reacting impulsively.

Focus on the Process: Shift your focus from the outcome of individual trades to the process of executing your trading plan effectively. Emphasise disciplined and patient trading rather than chasing quick profits.

Limit Information Overload: Avoid overloading yourself with too much market information or constantly monitoring price movements. Set specific times for market analysis and trading activities to maintain focus and prevent impulsive behaviour.

Learn from Mistakes: Embrace the learning process and view mistakes as opportunities for growth. Analyse your trading decisions and outcomes to identify areas for improvement and adjust your approach accordingly.

Practice Self-Care: Take breaks from trading to rest and recharge both mentally and physically. Engage in activities outside of trading that bring you joy and relaxation, such as spending time with loved ones or pursuing hobbies.

Summary

Patience is a valuable trait in trading that can lead to better decision-making, improved emotional resilience, and greater long-term success. By developing a solid trading plan, practising delayed gratification, setting realistic goals, cultivating mindfulness, focusing on the process, limiting information overload, learning from mistakes, and practising self-care, traders can strengthen their patience and enhance their trading performance over time. Remember that patience is not just about waiting; it's about maintaining discipline and composure in the face of uncertainty and adversity.

9. POSITIVE AFFIRMATIONS

Positive affirmations can be a powerful tool in trading to cultivate a strong, confident, and disciplined mindset. By regularly practising affirmations, traders can reinforce positive beliefs, reduce anxiety, and improve their overall mental resilience. Here are some effective positive affirmations for traders, along with how to incorporate them into your daily routine:

Positive Affirmations for Traders

"I am a disciplined and patient trader."

Reinforces the importance of discipline and patience, essential qualities for successful trading.

"I make decisions based on my trading plan, not emotions."

Emphasises sticking to a well-defined trading strategy and avoiding emotional decision-making.

"I manage risk effectively and protect my capital."

Highlights the importance of risk management and capital preservation.

"I learn and grow from every trade, whether it's a win or a loss."

Encourages a growth mindset, viewing every trade as a learning opportunity.

"I trust my analysis and strategy."

Builds confidence in your trading plan and analytical skills.

"I remain calm and composed, regardless of market conditions."

Promotes emotional stability and reduces stress during volatile market situations.

"I am focused and dedicated to improving my trading skills."

Reinforces commitment to continuous learning and improvement.

"I accept losses as a natural part of trading and move on without dwelling on them."

Helps in managing the emotional impact of losses and maintaining a forward-looking perspective.

"I am in control of my trading decisions and actions."

Empowers you to take responsibility for your trading outcomes.

"I celebrate my successes and acknowledge my progress."

Encourages positive reinforcement and recognition of achievements.

How to Incorporate Affirmations into Your Routine:

Daily Practice

Set aside a few minutes each morning and evening to repeat your affirmations. Consistency is key to reinforcing these positive beliefs.

Written Affirmations

Write your affirmations in a journal or on sticky notes placed around your trading area. Seeing them regularly will help embed them in your subconscious mind.

Visualization

Combine affirmations with visualization techniques. Imagine yourself executing trades successfully, adhering to your plan, and remaining calm under pressure while repeating your affirmations.

Affirmations as Mantras

Use affirmations as mantras during your trading sessions, especially in stressful moments. Repeating them can help you stay focused and composed.

Mindfulness and Meditation

Integrate affirmations into mindfulness or meditation practices. This can enhance their impact by helping you stay present and centred.

Record and Listen

Record your affirmations and listen to them regularly, especially during activities like commuting or exercising. This reinforces the positive messages throughout your day.

Positive Environment

Surround yourself with a supportive trading community or mentor who reinforces positive attitudes and behaviours.

Summary

Positive affirmations can significantly influence your trading mindset and performance by fostering discipline, confidence, and emotional stability. By regularly practising and internalising these affirmations, you can build a resilient and positive mental framework that supports your trading goals. Remember, the key to effective affirmations is consistency and genuine belief in the messages you are reinforcing.

10. VISUALIZATION TECHNIQUES

Visualization is a powerful mental technique that can help traders improve performance, enhance focus, and build confidence. By vividly imagining successful trading scenarios and positive outcomes, traders can prepare their minds for real-world trading situations. Here's how to effectively incorporate visualization into your trading routine:

Benefits of Visualization in Trading

Mental Rehearsal: Visualization allows you to mentally rehearse trading scenarios, which can help you respond more effectively when similar situations arise in real life.

Confidence Building: Seeing yourself successfully executing trades and sticking to your plan can boost your confidence and reduce anxiety.

Emotional Control: Visualizing calm and composed reactions to market volatility can help you manage stress and emotions during actual trading.

Focus and Discipline: Regular visualization helps reinforce your trading plan and strategies, promoting discipline and adherence to your rules.

Goal Setting: Imagining achieving your trading goals can motivate you and provide a clear sense of direction.

How to Practice Visualization

Create a Quiet Environment: Find a quiet place where you won't be disturbed. This will help you focus and fully engage in the visualization process.

Relax and Clear Your Mind: Sit comfortably, close your eyes, and take a few deep breaths to relax your body and clear your mind of distractions.

Visualize Specific Scenarios

Winning Trades: Imagine yourself identifying a high-probability setup, entering the trade, and watching it move in your favour. Visualize the emotions of satisfaction and confidence as you close the trade for a profit.

Losing Trades: Picture yourself experiencing a loss but handling it calmly and professionally. See yourself analyzing the loss, learning from it, and moving on without emotional turmoil.

Incorporate Sensory Details: Engage all your senses to make the visualization vivid. Imagine the look of your trading platform, the sound of market updates, and the feel of your mouse or keyboard as you execute trades.

Focus on the Process: Emphasize the process of trading rather than just the outcomes. Visualize yourself following your trading plan, conducting analysis, setting stop-loss and take-profit orders, and sticking to your strategy.

Positive Outcomes: See yourself achieving your trading goals, whether it's hitting a specific profit target, maintaining discipline, or executing a perfect trade. Feel the emotions of success and accomplishment.

Consistency and Routine: Practice visualization regularly, ideally as part of your daily routine. Consistency helps reinforce the positive mental patterns you're developing.

Combine with Affirmations: Use positive affirmations during your visualization sessions. For example, while visualizing a successful trade, repeat affirmations like "I am a disciplined trader" or "I execute my trades with confidence."

Example Visualization Exercise

Morning Routine

Spend 5-10 minutes each morning visualizing your trading day.

See yourself calmly analyzing the market, identifying trade setups, and executing trades according to your plan.

Visualize handling both winning and losing trades with emotional stability.

Pre-Trade Preparation

Before starting your trading session, take a few minutes to visualize the specific trades you're planning to take.

Imagine the market movements, your entry and exit points, and your reaction to different scenarios.

End-of-Day Review

At the end of the trading day, visualize reviewing your trades and analyzing what went well and what didn't.

See yourself learning from your experiences and feeling motivated to improve.

Summary

Visualization is a powerful technique that can enhance your trading performance by building confidence, reinforcing discipline, and preparing your mind for various trading scenarios. By incorporating regular visualization practices into your trading routine, you can develop a more resilient and focused mindset, ultimately leading to more consistent and successful trading outcomes.

Chapter 6

OVERTRADING

INTRODUCTION AND CHARACTERISTICS OF OVERTRADING

Introduction

Overtrading in the context of trading refers to the excessive buying and selling of securities. Most of the novice traders lose money due to this overtrading. Every day, 2 or 3 trades are more than enough to make huge money from the stock market. It is characterised by making frequent trades that are often unnecessary and not based on a solid strategy or market analysis. Overtrading can result from a trader's impulsive behaviour, emotional reactions, or a misunderstanding of market conditions, leading to higher transaction costs and potential financial losses.

CHARACTERISTICS OF OVERTRADING

High Trading Frequency

Making a significantly larger number of trades than usual or necessary.

Engaging in trades without substantial market movement or new information.

Emotional Decision-Making

Allowing emotions such as fear, greed, or excitement to drive trading decisions.

Reacting impulsively to market fluctuations rather than following a predetermined plan.

Lack of Strategic Planning

Trading without a clear plan or strategy.

Ignoring or frequently changing trading strategies without thorough analysis.

Increased Transaction Costs

Accumulating high fees and commissions due to the large volume of trades.

Neglecting the impact of transaction costs on overall profitability.

Inadequate Risk Management

Failing to set or adhere to stop-loss orders and risk limits.

Taking on excessive risk in an attempt to recover from losses.

Burnout and Fatigue

Experiencing mental and emotional exhaustion from constant monitoring and trading.

Suffering from decreased decision-making quality due to fatigue.

Reduced Focus on Quality Trades

Overlooking high-quality trading opportunities due to the focus on quantity.

Making trades based on marginal setups rather than strong, well-analysed signals.

Short-Term Focus

Prioritizing short-term gains over long-term investment goals.

Frequent switching between trades to capture minor price movements.

Understanding these characteristics can help traders identify and address overtrading behaviour, ultimately leading to more disciplined and profitable trading practices.

Psychological Factors Leading to Overtrading

Fear of Missing Out (FOMO)

Definition: The anxiety that an exciting or interesting event may currently be happening elsewhere, often aroused by posts seen on social media.

Impact on Trading: Traders may rush into trades without proper analysis because they fear missing profitable opportunities others might be capitalising on. This can lead to impulsive and frequent trading.

Impulse Control Issues

Definition: Difficulty in resisting the urge to take immediate action.

Impact on Trading: Traders may find it hard to stick to their trading plan and instead make **trades on a whim, driven by sudden urges or market movements.**

Overconfidence

Definition: Having an inflated belief in one's own abilities or judgement.

Impact on Trading: Traders may overestimate their market knowledge and abilities, leading them to trade excessively, believing they can predict market movements accurately.

Recency Bias

Definition: The tendency to give undue importance to recent events or information.

Impact on Trading: Traders might overtrade based on recent market trends or outcomes, disregarding long-term data and overall market conditions.

Loss Aversion

Definition: The tendency to prefer avoiding losses rather than acquiring equivalent gains.

Impact on Trading: Traders may engage in overtrading to quickly recover from losses, often leading to even greater losses as they take on riskier positions without adequate analysis.

Adrenaline Rush and Thrill-Seeking

Definition: The excitement or stimulation experienced during high-risk activities.

Impact on Trading: Some traders might get addicted to the thrill of making frequent trades, akin to gambling, and end up overtrading for the sake of the adrenaline rush rather than rational decision-making.

Confirmation Bias

Definition: The tendency to search for, interpret, favour, and recall information in a way that confirms one's preexisting beliefs.

Impact on Trading: Traders may overtrade based on information that supports their current market outlook while ignoring contradicting data, leading to unbalanced and excessive trading.

Chasing Losses

Definition: Attempting to recover losses by making more trades, often with increasing desperation.

Impact on Trading: After a losing trade, traders might make more trades in quick succession to try and recoup their losses, often leading to a cycle of continuous trading and further losses.

Social Pressure and Herd Mentality

Definition: The influence of the majority on an individual's decisions.

Impact on Trading: Traders might follow the actions of others, engaging in trades because they see others doing so rather than based on their own analysis, leading to overtrading.

Perfectionism

Definition: The desire to achieve flawlessness and set excessively high-performance standards.

Impact on Trading: Traders might constantly tweak and change their positions in an attempt to optimize every trade perfectly, resulting in excessive trading activity.

Understanding these psychological factors can help traders recognize and mitigate the underlying causes of overtrading, leading to more disciplined and effective trading behaviour.

FINANCIAL CONSEQUENCES OF OVERTRADING

Increased Transaction Costs

Definition: Higher expenses due to frequent buying and selling.

Impact: Each trade incurs fees such as commissions, spreads, and taxes. Over time, these costs can significantly reduce net profits, especially for traders with small profit margins per trade.

Erosion of Capital

Definition: Gradual depletion of trading capital.

Impact: Continuous trading, particularly when decisions are driven by emotions or poor judgement, can lead to repeated losses. Over time, this can deplete the trader's capital, reducing the ability to take advantage of future opportunities.

Reduced Profitability

Definition: Decreased overall returns from trading activities.

Impact: Overtrading can lead to suboptimal trades that do not align with a sound strategy. This results in lower average returns and potentially turns profitable strategies into unprofitable ones.

Diminished Return on Investment (ROI)

Definition: Lower efficiency in generating profits from invested capital.

Impact: With high transaction costs and frequent trading losses, the ROI diminishes. This makes it harder to achieve financial goals and reduces the compounding effect of gains over time.

Tax Implications

Definition: Higher tax liabilities due to frequent trading.

Impact: Short-term trades are often taxed at higher rates than long-term investments. Frequent trading can lead to a larger tax burden, further eating into net returns.

Opportunity Cost

Definition: The loss of potential gains from other opportunities due to capital being tied up in frequent trades.

Impact: Overtrading can result in missed opportunities as capital is constantly deployed in short-term trades rather than being invested in more promising, longer-term opportunities.

Psychological and Emotional Strain

Definition: Mental and emotional stress caused by continuous trading activities.

Impact: Although not directly financial, the stress and fatigue from overtrading can lead to poor decision-making, further compounding financial losses. The psychological burden can also affect overall well-being and productivity.

Margin and Leverage Risks

Definition: Increased exposure to financial instruments that amplify gains and losses.

Impact: Traders who use margin and leverage excessively risk magnifying their losses. In cases of rapid market movements against their positions, they may face margin calls, leading to forced liquidations and significant financial setbacks.

Understanding these financial consequences is crucial for traders to recognise the importance of disciplined trading practices and the long-term benefits of avoiding overtrading.

IMPACT OF OVERTRADING ON TRADING PERFORMANCE

Decreased Decision-Making Quality

Impact: Frequent trading can lead to rushed and impulsive decisions. When traders are constantly engaged in the market, they may not have adequate time to thoroughly analyse each trade, resulting in poorer decision quality and increased errors.

Increased Psychological Stress

Impact: The constant need to monitor and execute trades can cause significant mental strain and stress. This heightened stress can impair cognitive functions, reduce concentration, and negatively affect judgement, leading to suboptimal trading performance.

Lower Win Rate

Impact: Overtrading often involves entering trades based on less reliable signals or without proper analysis. This can result in a lower win rate as the quality of trade setups diminishes. Poorer trade selection typically leads to more frequent losses.

Reduced Focus on High-Probability Trades

Impact: By making numerous trades, traders may divert their attention from high-probability setups to less favourable ones. This shift in focus can lead to missing out on better opportunities that align with their trading strategy, thereby reducing overall profitability.

Impaired Risk Management

Impact: Overtrading can lead to inconsistent risk management practices. Traders might overextend their risk exposure, ignore stop-loss levels, or take larger positions than warranted. Poor risk management increases the likelihood of significant losses.

Emotional Trading

Impact: Overtrading often stems from emotional impulses rather than rational analysis. Emotional trading can lead to a cycle of revenge trading (trying to recover losses) or greed-driven trading (trying to maximize gains), both of which can be detrimental to performance.

Volatility in Performance

Impact: Overtrading can cause performance to become highly volatile, with large swings in profit and loss. This volatility can be destabilizing and make it difficult to maintain a consistent trading record, which is crucial for long-term success.

Understanding these impacts can help traders recognize the importance of maintaining discipline, sticking to a well-defined trading strategy, and avoiding the pitfalls of overtrading. By doing so, they can enhance their overall trading performance and achieve more consistent, sustainable results.

STRATEGIES TO AVOID OVERTRADING

Develop and Stick to a Trading Plan

Definition: A trading plan is a comprehensive blueprint that outlines your trading strategy, including entry and exit criteria, risk management rules, and specific goals.

Implementation: Create a detailed plan before you start trading and adhere to it strictly. The plan should define the maximum number of trades per day or week, the criteria for entering and exiting trades, and the maximum amount of capital at risk for each trade.

Set Clear Goals and Limits

Definition: Establishing specific objectives and boundaries for your trading activities.

Implementation: Define daily, weekly, and monthly profit and loss targets. Set a limit on the number of trades you will execute within a specific time frame to avoid overtrading. For example, limit yourself to a maximum of 3 trades per day. After reaching the limit close your trading terminal and leave the room and do any other activities like book reading, watching movies, listen music etc.

Use Stop-Loss Orders

Definition: A stop-loss order is an instruction to close a position when it reaches a certain level of loss.

Implementation: Always set stop-loss orders to protect your capital from significant losses. This ensures you automatically exit a trade if it moves against you, preventing emotional decision-making and minimizing risk.

Implement Position Sizing Techniques

Definition: Position sizing refers to determining the amount of capital to invest in a single trade.

Implementation: Use position sizing rules, such as the 1% or 2% rule, where you risk only a small percentage of your trading capital on any single trade. This helps manage risk and prevents substantial losses from any one trade.

Maintain a Trading Journal

Definition: A trading journal is a record of all your trades, including details about why you made each trade and its outcome.

Implementation: Regularly update your trading journal with information about each trade, including the reasoning behind it, entry and exit points, and the results. Reviewing your journal can help you identify patterns of overtrading and areas for improvement.

Automate Your Trading

Definition: Using automated trading systems or algorithms to execute trades based on predefined criteria.

Implementation: Develop or use automated trading systems that follow your trading plan and strategy. Automation can help remove emotional biases and ensure that you adhere to your trading rules without making impulsive decisions.

Use Technical Indicators and Alerts

Definition: Technical indicators are tools used to analyze market conditions and generate trading signals.

Implementation: Utilize technical indicators to set up alerts for potential trading opportunities. Alerts can help you avoid constantly monitoring the market and making impulsive trades. Stick to trades that meet your predefined criteria based on these indicators.

Adopt a Long-Term Perspective

Definition: Focusing on long-term trading goals rather than short-term gains.

Implementation: Shift your focus from trying to make quick profits to achieving consistent, long-term success. Avoid the temptation to enter trades without solid analysis or based on short-term market fluctuations.

Manage Emotional Responses

Definition: Techniques to control emotional reactions that may lead to impulsive trading.

Implementation: Practice mindfulness, meditation, or other stress-relief techniques to manage emotions. Take breaks from trading to avoid burnout and maintain a clear, objective mindset.

By incorporating these risk management strategies, traders can avoid the pitfalls of overtrading, protect their capital, and enhance their overall trading performance.

Educate Yourself and Practice Mindfulness

Action: Continuously educate yourself about trading, market analysis, and risk management. Practice mindfulness and stress-reduction techniques to maintain emotional control.

Implementation: Enroll in trading courses, read books, and follow reputable financial news sources to enhance your trading knowledge. Incorporate mindfulness practices such as meditation, yoga, or regular breaks to manage stress and maintain a clear, focused mindset.

By following this action plan, traders can systematically address overtrading, improve their trading performance, and achieve long-term success in the markets.

Chapter 7

Trading Journal

INTRODUCTION TO TRADING JOURNALS

Definition and Purpose

A trading journal is a detailed record of all trading activities, including the rationale behind each trade, execution details, outcomes, and the trader's emotional state during each transaction. It serves as a crucial tool for traders of all experience levels to track their performance, analyze their trading behavior, and make informed decisions to enhance their strategies.

The primary purpose of maintaining a trading journal is to foster discipline and consistency in trading. By systematically documenting every trade, traders can identify strengths and weaknesses in their strategies, recognize recurring patterns, and gain insights into their psychological responses to market events. A trading journal acts as both a logbook and a learning tool, helping traders refine their approaches and achieve long-term success in the financial markets.

BENEFITS OF MAINTAINING A TRADING JOURNAL

Enhanced Self-Discipline: A trading journal enforces accountability and encourages traders to adhere to their strategies and risk management rules. By recording trades, traders can evaluate whether they are following their plan or deviating due to impulsive decisions.

Performance Tracking: Keeping a detailed record allows traders to assess their performance over time. Metrics such as win rate, average profit/loss per trade, and risk-reward ratios can be calculated and analyzed to understand overall trading effectiveness.

Pattern Recognition: By reviewing historical trades, traders can identify patterns in their trading behaviour and market setups that consistently lead to profits or losses. This insight can be used to optimize future trades.

Emotional Awareness: Documenting the emotional state during trades helps traders understand how emotions like fear, greed, or overconfidence affect their decisions. Recognizing these influences is the first step in managing them effectively.

Strategy Refinement: A trading journal provides valuable data that can be used to evaluate and refine trading strategies. Traders can test different approaches and assess their impact on performance, allowing for continuous improvement.

Learning and Growth: Regularly updating and reviewing a trading journal fosters a habit of reflection and learning. It encourages traders to think critically about their decisions and develop a deeper understanding of market dynamics.

History and Evolution of Trading Journals

Trading journals have been an integral part of successful trading for centuries. Early traders kept handwritten logs of their trades, noting down prices, market conditions, and personal observations. As financial markets and trading strategies evolved, so did the methods for maintaining trading records.

With the advent of personal computers and spreadsheet software in the late 20th century, traders began using digital tools to track their activities. This allowed for more detailed analysis and easier data manipulation. The rise of the internet and advancements in technology further transformed trading journals, making them more sophisticated and accessible.

Today, a wide range of specialized trading journal software and apps are available, offering features such as automated data entry, advanced analytics, and integration with trading platforms. These modern tools provide traders with powerful capabilities to analyze their performance, identify trends, and continuously improve their strategies.

Why Every Trader Needs a Trading Journal

Regardless of whether you are a novice or an experienced trader, maintaining a trading journal is essential for achieving consistent profitability. The process of documenting and analysing trades provides invaluable insights that cannot be gained through observation alone. A trading journal helps bridge the gap between theoretical knowledge and practical application, allowing traders to learn from their experiences and avoid repeating mistakes.

In the fast-paced and often unpredictable world of trading, a journal serves as an anchor, keeping traders grounded and focused on their long-term goals. By fostering discipline, enhancing self-awareness, and promoting continuous learning, a trading journal is an indispensable tool for anyone serious about succeeding in the financial markets.

In the following chapters, we will delve into the specifics of setting up a trading journal, documenting trades, analyzing performance, and using insights to refine trading strategies. Whether you are just starting out or looking to enhance your existing trading practices, this guide will provide you with the knowledge and tools to make the most of your trading journal.

Setting Up Your Trading Journal

Creating an effective trading journal is a crucial step toward improving your trading performance. A well-structured journal provides a comprehensive view of your trading activities, helping you make informed decisions and refine your strategies. Here's a detailed guide on setting up your trading journal.

Choosing the Right Format

Physical Notebook:

Pros: Tangible, no reliance on technology, easy to personalize.

Cons: Limited analytical capabilities, time-consuming to update and review.

Best For Traders who prefer a hands-on approach and enjoy writing manually.

Spreadsheets:

Pros: Flexible, customizable, powerful analytical functions, easy to update.

Cons: It requires basic knowledge of spreadsheet software, and it can become cumbersome with large data sets.

Best For Traders who are comfortable with Excel or Google Sheets and want a balance between customization and functionality.

Specialized Software:

Pros: Automated data entry, advanced analytics, integration with trading platforms, user-friendly interfaces.

Cons: It can be expensive and may have a learning curve that is dependent on software updates and support.

Best For Traders who want comprehensive features and automation to streamline their journaling process.

Examples: Edgewonk, TraderSync, Tradervue.

By setting up a comprehensive trading journal and consistently updating it, you can gain valuable insights into your trading performance, develop greater self-discipline, and make data-driven decisions that enhance your overall success in the markets.

DOCUMENTING TRADES

Effective documentation of trades is critical for improving your trading performance. A well-maintained trading journal captures detailed information about each trade, providing valuable insights for the analysis and refinement of your trading strategies. Here's a comprehensive guide to documenting trades for your book.

1. Trade Details

a. Date and Time:

Entry and Exit Date and Time: Record the exact date and time when you entered and Exit the trade. This helps correlate the trade with market conditions at that specific moment.

b. Asset Traded:

Specify the financial instrument involved in the trade (e.g., stock, indices, options, forex pair, commodity, cryptocurrency). Include the ticker symbol or currency pair code.

c. Trade Direction:

Indicate whether the trade was a long (buy) or short (sell) position. This helps in assessing your market bias and strategy effectiveness.

d. Entry and Exit Prices:

Entry Price: Document the price at which you entered the trade.

Exit Price: Note the price at which you exited the trade. This information is essential for calculating profit or loss.

2. Position Size

a. Quantity:

Record the number of shares, contracts, or lots traded. This helps you understand the scale of your trade and its impact on your portfolio.

b. Total Value:

Calculate the total value of the position by multiplying the entry price by the quantity traded. This provides context on the size of your trade.

3. Trade Rationale

a. Technical Analysis:

Indicators Used: List the technical indicators that influenced your decision (e.g., moving averages, RSI, CPR).

Chart Patterns: Describe any chart patterns observed (e.g., head and shoulders, double top/bottom).

Support and Resistance Levels: Note key support and resistance levels that played a role in your trade.

b. Fundamental Analysis:

Economic Data: Include relevant economic reports or data releases (e.g., GDP, employment figures).

Company News: Document significant news related to the company or asset (e.g., earnings reports, product launches).

c. Market Conditions:

Overall Market Trend: Describe the broader market environment (e.g., bullish, bearish, sideways).

Volatility: Note the level of market volatility and any unusual events (e.g., geopolitical events, natural disasters).

4. Risk Management

a. Stop-Loss Level:

Record the stop-loss price set to limit potential losses. This shows your risk management approach and discipline.

b. Take-Profit Level:

Note the take-profit price, if any, set to secure gains. This indicates your target profit level for the trade.

c. Risk-Reward Ratio:

Calculate and document the risk-reward ratio for the trade. This helps in assessing whether the trade had a favourable risk-reward profile.

5. Outcome

a. Profit or Loss:

Amount: Record the total profit or loss from the trade in monetary terms.

Percentage Return: Calculate the return as a percentage of the capital at risk. This helps in comparing the performance of different trades.

6. Emotional State

a. Before the Trade:

Note your emotional state before entering the trade (e.g., confident, anxious, excited). This helps in understanding how pre-trade emotions impact your decisions.

b. During the Trade:

Record significant emotions experienced while the trade was open (e.g., fear, greed, patience). This provides insight into your emotional response to market movements.

c. After the Trade:

Reflect on your emotions after closing the trade (e.g., satisfied, regretful, relieved). This helps in assessing the impact of emotions on your trading performance.

7. Notes and Observations

a. Market Events:

Document any significant market events or news that occurred during the trade. This provides context for unexpected price movements.

b. Personal Observations:

Include any personal insights or lessons learned from the trade. This could be anything from noticing a recurring pattern to realising a mistake.

c.   Strategy Adjustments:

Note any adjustments you plan to make to your trading strategy based on the trade's outcome. This shows your commitment to continuous improvement.

Notes and Observations

Market Events: No significant events

Personal Observations: The moving average crossover strategy worked well in this instance. Need to be cautious of price dips before upward movement.

Strategy Adjustments: Consider setting a slightly wider stop-loss to accommodate minor price dips.

By meticulously documenting trades in this manner, traders can gain deeper insights into their performance, identify areas for improvement, and refine their strategies for better results.

Analyzing Your Trading Performance

Analyzing your trading performance is a crucial step toward improving as a trader. By reviewing past trades, identifying strengths and weaknesses, and making data-driven decisions, you can refine your strategies and increase your profitability. Here's how to effectively analyse your trading performance for your book:

1.   Reviewing Trades

a.   Regular Review Sessions:

Schedule regular sessions to review your trades. Weekly or monthly reviews are common, but the frequency depends on your trading style and activity level.

b.   Comprehensive Analysis:

Review each trade systematically, considering various factors such as entry and exit points, trade rationale, risk management, and emotional state.

c.   Learn from Both Wins and Losses:

Analyze both winning and losing trades. Winning trades can reinforce effective strategies while losing trades provide valuable lessons.

2.   Performance Metrics

a.   Win Rate:

Calculate your win rate by dividing the number of winning trades by the total number of trades. This indicates the percentage of trades that result in a profit.

b.   Risk-Reward Ratio:

Evaluate your risk-reward ratio by dividing the average gain per winning trade by the average loss per losing trade. A ratio greater than 1 indicates a favourable risk-reward profile.

c.   Average Profit/Loss per Trade:

Calculate the average profit or loss per trade to assess the overall profitability of your trading strategy.

8. Keep a Trading Journal

Record Observations: Document your observations and insights from analyzing patterns and trends in your trading journal. Note down which patterns have been consistently profitable and which have not.

Track Changes Over Time: Monitor how patterns and trends evolve over time. What worked in the past may not work in the future, so it's essential to adapt and refine your strategies accordingly.

Improving Trading Strategies

Improving trading strategies is an ongoing process that involves analysing past performance, identifying areas for enhancement, and implementing changes to increase profitability and reduce risk. Here are steps to effectively improve your trading strategies:

1. Review Historical Performance

Analyze Trade Data: Review your historical trades to identify patterns, strengths, and weaknesses in your trading strategy.

Assess Performance Metrics: Evaluate key performance metrics such as win rate, risk-reward ratio, and average profit/loss per trade to understand the overall effectiveness of your strategy.

Identify Successful Trades: Identify trades that have consistently yielded profits and analyze the factors contributing to their success.

2. Identify Areas for Improvement

Recognize Weaknesses: Identify weaknesses or shortcomings in your current trading strategy, such as frequent losses, low win rates, or inconsistent performance.

Understand Mistakes: Analyze losing trades to understand the reasons behind the losses. Common mistakes may include poor risk management, emotional trading, or lack of discipline.

Spot Missed Opportunities: Look for missed trading opportunities or setups that your strategy failed to capitalize on. Determine if there are any adjustments needed to exploit these opportunities in the future.

3. Refine Entry and Exit Criteria

Fine-Tune Entry Signals: Refine your entry criteria based on your analysis of past trades. Look for specific technical indicators, chart patterns, or fundamental factors that have reliably signalled profitable trades.

Optimize Exit Strategy: Evaluate different exit strategies, such as setting profit targets or trailing stop-loss orders, to maximize profits while minimizing losses. Experiment with different approaches to find the most effective one for your strategy.

4. Enhance Risk Management

Review Risk Management Rules: Assess your risk management rules and determine if they are effectively protecting your capital. Consider adjusting position sizes, stop-loss levels, or overall risk exposure to better manage risk.

Implement Stop-Loss Orders: Ensure that every trade has a well-defined stop-loss level to limit potential losses. Adjust stop-loss levels based on market conditions and volatility to maintain an appropriate risk-reward ratio.

5. Adapt to Market Conditions

Stay Flexible: Recognize that market conditions are constantly changing, and no single strategy works in all market environments. Be prepared to adapt your strategy to different market conditions, such as trending or ranging markets.

Diversify Strategies: Consider diversifying your trading strategies to take advantage of various market conditions. Develop strategies for different asset classes, timeframes, or trading styles to spread risk and increase opportunities.

6. Back-test and Validate Changes

Back-test Modifications: Back-test any changes or enhancements to your trading strategy using historical data to validate their effectiveness. Ensure that the modifications improve overall performance and profitability.

Paper Trade: Practice trading the refined strategy in a simulated or paper trading environment to test its performance in real-time market conditions without risking capital.

7. Monitor and Adjust

Continuously Monitor Performance: Regularly monitor the performance of your refined trading strategy in live market conditions. Keep detailed records of trades and performance metrics to track progress over time.

Adjust as Needed: Be prepared to make further adjustments to your strategy based on ongoing analysis and market feedback. Trading strategies should evolve and adapt to changing market dynamics to remain effective.

By following these steps and continuously refining your trading strategies, you can increase your chances of success in the financial markets and achieve more consistent and profitable trading results over time.

End Note

As we come to the end of Unlock the Secrets of the Share Market; A Strategic Guide to Trading Success, it's important to reflect on the journey and the transformation that you, as a trader, have undertaken. Day trading is not just about understanding the markets and executing trades; it is a holistic endeavour that encompasses technical knowledge, strategic planning, psychological resilience, and continuous learning.

Embrace Continuous Learning

The financial markets are dynamic and ever-evolving. What works today might not work tomorrow, and staying ahead requires a commitment to continuous education and adaptation. Stay curious, seek out new information, and be willing to refine your strategies as market conditions change. Attend seminars, read the latest books, follow market analysts, and never stop expanding your knowledge base.

Develop a Growth Mindset

Success in day trading comes with its share of challenges and setbacks. Developing a growth mindset is essential. View mistakes and losses as learning opportunities rather than failures. Analyze your trades meticulously, understand what went wrong, and use those insights to improve your future performance. Resilience and the ability to adapt are the hallmarks of successful traders.

Maintain Discipline and Emotional Control

The importance of discipline and emotional control cannot be overstated. Day trading can be emotionally taxing, with its rapid pace and high stakes. Establish a trading plan, stick to it, and avoid impulsive decisions driven by fear or greed. Practice techniques such as mindfulness and stress management to maintain a clear and focused mind during trading sessions.

Prioritize Risk Management

Protecting your capital is paramount. No matter how promising a trade setup might look, always prioritize risk management. Use stop-loss orders, define your risk-reward ratio, and never risk more than a small percentage of your trading capital on a single trade. Consistent risk management is what will ensure your longevity in the trading arena.

Cultivate a Supportive Network

Surround yourself with a supportive network of fellow traders, mentors, and industry experts. Engaging with a community can provide invaluable insights, moral support, and a platform to share experiences and strategies. Learning from others and sharing your knowledge in return creates a symbiotic environment that fosters growth and improvement.

Stay Passionate and Patient

Passion for trading will keep you motivated through the highs and lows. Stay enthusiastic about the markets and the process of trading. Patience is equally crucial—understand that mastery takes time, and consistent effort will eventually yield results. Celebrate small victories and milestones along the way to keep your motivation high.

Looking Ahead

The road to day trading mastery is a continuous journey rather than a destination. As you apply the principles and strategies outlined in this book, remember that success in trading is a blend of art and science.

Cultivate your intuition while grounding your decisions in sound analysis and strategy.

We hope this book has provided you with a solid foundation and valuable insights into the world of day trading. As you continue on your trading journey, may you achieve not only financial success but also personal growth and fulfilment. The skills you have developed here will serve you well in navigating the markets and making informed, confident trading decisions.

Thank you for choosing Unlock the Secrets of the Share Market; A Strategic Guide to Trading Success as your companion in this exciting endeavour. We wish you the best of luck and continued success in your trading career.

"Quitters Never Win

Winners Never Quit"